THE ULTIMATE CHALLENGE

By:
CHARLES LUNA

Copyright © 2014 Charles Luna

All rights reserved.

ISBN-10: 1499559879

ISBN-13: 9781499559873

Acknowledgements

I would like to thank my two boys, Will and Drew for helping me with the design of this book. I would also like to thank my college housemates without whom this story would have never been written. Last but not least, thanks to my loyal readers. I hope that you enjoy this story.

The Ultimate Challenge is Charles Luna's third book. He has also written –

The Ticket

The New World Project

To read about or purchase his previous books please visit www.Lunanovels.com

Chapter I

Thursday February 17th, 2014. 3:30 p.m. North Richland Hills, Texas

"Look who's here!" my wife said to our 18 month old son. She was getting home from work after picking our son Thomas up from daycare. Thomas was always excited to see me when they got home. Today was different. Instead of jumping up to hold him, I just stared straight ahead, looking at nothing in particular. My wife Susan automatically knew that something was wrong.

"Mark, what is it?" Susan asked with fear in her voice.

After ten seconds of silence I answered "I received a phone call that John Simmons died last night of cancer. He had a brain tumor that doctors found two months ago – way too late."

"I'm sorry sweetie. Are you okay?" Susan asked with compassion in her voice.

"I'm fine, just stunned."

John Simmons was a friend from college. We both spent four years together at Berry College in Rome, Georgia. In college, we had lived together in a house with three other guys. John and I had lost touch over the years. It was easy to keep up with him on television though because he was one of the wealthiest men in the country. He earned his wealth by moving to Napa Valley at the beginning of the Tech Boom. He developed three different start-up companies and sold each very quickly before the cash dried up for start-ups. John was no genius, but he was a very likeable guy with a strong work ethic and a good sense of opportunity. He was the picture of health, a great athlete and outdoorsman. The thing that made the news of his death so shocking was that he was only thirty years old.

My name is Mark Holland. My wife and I moved to the Fort Worth area four years ago because I was offered a job as a salesman for Worth Sports, a baseball company that I had always wanted to work for. We live a nice life, we bought a house two years ago and we have an eighteen month old son named Thomas. My wife, Susan, is very beautiful and extremely intelligent. We started dating after reuniting at a high school reunion and were married a year and a half later. She is an office manager for an orthodontist. Thomas is a beautiful kid. He is just starting to talk and has really started to develop his personality. He is the happiest baby that you will ever meet. When he wakes up he is smiling and always ready for a new day to begin.

"I guess we need to start making arrangements to drive to Georgia" I said.

Susan replied "I'll call Dr. Sellers and let him know."

We arrived in Alpharetta, Georgia late Friday afternoon. It was freezing cold but we dodged the predicted snowstorms on our trip. We went straight to our hotel which was only about five miles from the funeral home. It was amazing for me to see the growth that had occurred around Atlanta over the last few years. The sprawling countryside that leads to the beautiful north Georgia Mountains had become one big cement pond. A six lane highway had brought people with it as business after business and neighborhood after neighborhood had been built with the lure of the mountains only being a short drive away.

I hate going to funeral homes but it is nothing new to me because I have had several friends and family members die throughout the years. I was both

THE ULTIMATE CHALLENGE

dreading it but also looking forward to seeing my friends at the same time. I would see my three closest friends – Jason, Eric and Drew. We were inseparable in college and still tried to keep in touch with each other.

I had directions to Moore funeral home. Visitation started at 5 so we showed up around 5:30. As we drove up to the funeral home, we were amazed at how many cars there were. John Simmons was famous in and around Atlanta. He was the second richest person in Georgia, with only Ted Turner having more wealth than John. He was single, his parents were dead and he was an only child. I couldn't help but wonder how many cars in the parking lot were people wanting to get a piece of his fortune. I never knew the rich John Simmons. While I still kept in touch with Jason, Eric and Drew, we all lost touch with John. His money didn't go to his head, but his business did consume his entire life. He started his company from his house with ten thousand dollars in cash and four years later, he was a billionaire. He struck while the iron was hot and got out of it faster than he got into it. I didn't expect to know many people at the funeral home but I was anxious to see my friends.

We entered the funeral home and as I expected my friends were congregated in the front lobby. Eric, Jason and Drew were all married but none had kids yet. After our greetings, Drew spoke up and said that we all had been asked to be pall bearers. It was good to see everyone but we were all quiet, still in shock that our friend was dead. After spending about twenty minutes in the lobby, Susan, Thomas and I went into the chapel. The flowers were overflowing into the pews. There were hundreds of arrangements that brightened up the dismal setting. The casket was closed with a single picture of John on top of it. After visiting the casket we awkwardly admired the flowers. A gentleman approached me and introduced himself as Ron Craig, John's attorney. When he figured out who I was he said "I have been making all of the arrangements for Mr. Simmons." He then said that he had been looking for me. "Mr. Simmons requested that I meet with you and his other three college house mates after his funeral. He spoke of you all many times. He wanted you to remember him as you knew him. That is why he didn't tell you that he was sick. He knew that he had a short time to live, so he arranged his funeral and tended to all of his business matters before his passing." I just stood there and nodded in agreement. Mr. Craig continued "After the funeral you and your friends can follow me to my office." I shook hands with the attorney and went to share the news with my friends. We were all uncomfortable in suits so we went back to the hotel and ordered pizza.

We bought a case of Miller Lite and before the first drink we toasted John Simmons. Everyone was curious as to what the meeting was about but it didn't consume our conversation. These few times together were our chance to revert back to our college days and reminisce about how stupid we were then.

I grew up with Jason Mulkey. We both went to Berry College to play baseball. An arm injury ended my college career before it ever really got started and Jason was cut from the team in a terrible decision by the coach. Jason was quiet and shy but very funny when you got to know him. He met his wife Kim in high school and she was the only girlfriend that he ever had. After being cut from the baseball team, Jason and I decided to take up partying as our hobby and that is when we met Eric and Drew.

Eric Jones is a football and wrestling coach. He is short and stocky with a short temper to go along with it. He is a newlywed. His wedding to his wife, Jessica, was the last time that the four of us were together about a year ago. Eric is a nice looking guy and he always had a lot of girlfriends in college. He spent the majority of his college career chasing women and drinking too much, just like the rest of us. Eric was a bit high strung but a lot of fun to be around. Jason and I became friends with him quickly because of our mutual love of sports.

We all met Drew about halfway through our freshman year at Berry. Drew is a people person. He could sell ice to an Eskimo and is always trying to find a way to get rich quick. He married his college sweetheart, Barbara. Drew is extremely laid back. To give you an idea about Drew's personality, the first day of our sophomore year in college he wanted to meet my parents. They are pretty

THE ULTIMATE CHALLENGE

conservative people and he knew that. He introduced himself to them wearing a t-shirt that said "Instant Asshole – Just Add Beer."

We spent the first thirty minutes catching up on each other's lives and discussing John's illness. Then after a few beers the old college stories started coming up. We told the same stories every time we got together because they always made us laugh. Somehow, we had all grown into mature and responsible adults. I rarely drank except when we all got together. In a way we were all glad that we had sewn our wild oats in college and lived to tell about it.

The stories went on for an hour or so until Drew brought up the topic of our meeting with the lawyer. "What do you guys think that meeting is about?" Drew asked.

I spoke up and said "I think John just wanted to say goodbye to us in a special way. His attorney told me that some of his high school friends will be there also."

"Oh great!" Eric sarcastically replied.

We all knew John's high school friends and none of us got along with them. We had met them twice. The first time we all had too much to drink and they picked a fight with us over something really trivial and they were staying at our house! John quickly stepped in that night and smoothed things over.

"Do you guys remember Pennant Fever?" Jason said with a grin on his face. We all just looked down and shook our heads. The second time that we met John's high school friends was at the beginning of our senior year in college. A few hours after they arrived, one of them got really sick – so sick that he crapped his pants. We found his underwear later in our back yard with the crap still in them. At the time, we didn't know what was wrong with the guy but over the course of the next two days everyone in the house was sick, either puking, crapping or both. The Braves were in the playoffs that weekend, hence the name Pennant Fever.

None of us knew what the meeting was about the next day but we could put up with a few rednecks for an hour to find out. It was after 12:00 A.M. and everyone was exhausted so we all went to our rooms and retired for the night.

Chapter 2

Saturday morning was freezing cold. It was twenty seven degrees outside when I woke up but the sky was clear and no bad weather was expected. Thomas woke up at his usual 6:30 time and he wanted to talk and run around. I have never been a morning person but Thomas is the one person in the world who can wake me up and I will be happy.

The funeral was scheduled for 12:00. We arrived at the funeral home at 11:00. As pall bearers, we went with the hearse from the funeral home to the cemetery where the funeral was to be held. As we drove up to the cemetery, we could see hundreds of cars and about a thousand people. By noon the temperature was up to forty degrees, still cold but bearable.

John Simmons funeral was like none other I have ever seen. As we carried his casket from the hearse to his grave, three bagpipe players played as everyone stood. The funeral included three speakers, a pastor and two business associates. Each speech was touching but the highlight came at the end of the funeral. After the last speaker, the bag pipers played "Amazing Grace" and then the pastor led everyone in singing the old hymn "I'll Fly Away." As we sang the chorus of the song, four F16 fighter jets flew by with a deafening roar and then pulled straight up into the air and disappeared into the sky. The hairs on my arms and neck stood straight up. John had definitely given each person at his funeral something to remember him for. Just as he had built his business, John was a master at endearing people to him.

CHARLES LUNA

After a stunned crowd paid their last respects, my friends and I piled into the Expedition to go to the lawyer's office. Our wives decided to go to lunch and then meet us back at the hotel after our meeting. We followed Ron Craig to his office, which was about twenty minutes away. We talked about the funeral for the entire twenty minutes. John had definitely gone out with a bang.

Ron Craig's office was in Buckhead, easily the most luxurious section of Atlanta. The drive took us by the Governor's mansion and we passed more mansions than we could count. Mr. Craig's office did not disappoint either. He worked in a high rise that looked fairly new. Outside of the office building, there was a large cement pond with a waterfall cascading down from the center on all four sides. As we followed Mr. Craig into the building, we were joined by John's high school friends. I would now describe them as refined rednecks. I recognized three of the four guys. They were friendly as were we, but no one remembered each other's names. I did recognize the "crapped his pants" guy. He looked a little embarrassed because I am sure he thought that he would never see us again.

Mr. Craig's office was extremely plush. The office housed three partners with two secretaries and two paralegals for each. The entrance to the offices was decorated with four very exotic looking plants and a very large salt water fish aquarium that was built into the wall. We followed a secretary directly to a conference room where a catered lunch was waiting for us. We spent about half an hour awkwardly eating lunch with the rednecks. The only thing that we had in common with these guys was a mutual friend so we kept the discussion on John Simmons. These guys looked more uncomfortable in suits than we did.

After lunch Mr. Craig joined us to begin the meeting. "Gentlemen, on behalf of Mr. Simmons I want to thank you all for coming here this afternoon. As John's attorney, I will be tending to all of his business matters. When he learned of his condition and that there was no chance for recovery, we made a video will and he gave me instructions as to how it should be administered. He will tell you the rest. Mr. Craig then opened two cabinet doors that revealed a large flat

THE ULTIMATE CHALLENGE

screened television. You could have heard a pin drop as the lawyer pushed the play button from his remote control.

John Simmons appeared sitting at his desk in his home with his Berry College degree framed behind him. "Well guys, if you are watching this, it means that I have gone on to a better place. I have brought you here today because with my death quickly approaching, I have taken some time to look back at my life. As you all know, my parents are gone and I was an only child. You guys are my only true friends. I have many people that ask me for money. Each of you has asked for nothing. My biggest regret is that I lost touch with each of you. My business has become my life. I have thoroughly enjoyed building my businesses but in return for my wealth, I have been unable to surround myself with friends who like me for me. As of now, I only have a couple of months to live and I will not be contacting any of you. I want you to remember me as being healthy. I want you to remember all of the great times that we had together. What I am about to tell you will change each of your lives forever. But I want you to remember one thing. Don't ever let money get in the way of your happiness and the people that you really care about. So here it goes.

The last will and testament of John L. Simmons, being of sound mind and body do hereby revoke all wills executed by me and dispose of my estate as follows. To my attorney Ron Craig, I leave a sum of one million dollars. I appoint Mr. Craig as executor of this will and grant him discretionary powers to administer this will. To various charities I leave ninety million dollars. Mr. Craig has all pertinent documents concerning the amount and name of each charity. To my eight friends in attendance here today, I have constructed "The Ultimate Challenge." Four of you will receive twenty five million dollars each. The other four will receive nothing. You will be divided into two teams of four. My college friends on one team and my high school friends on the other. The two teams will compete in The Ultimate Challenge with the first team to successfully complete the race declared the winner. This game will challenge you physically, mentally and emotionally. It will test your strength and your friendship with each other. This game will take you across this country and will last for several weeks. My hope is that this contest will be one of the greatest experiences of your lives, whether you win or lose. You may be wondering why I have decided to do this. There are several reasons. First, with only two months to live, I want to occupy my time planning the greatest event of my life. Secondly, all of you are very competitive and will enjoy this challenge. Third, I love drama and it's my money. Finally, the entire nation is going to enjoy this, the Expedition Channel has agreed to televise The Ultimate Challenge 24 hours per day from beginning to end.

There are a few details that I need to cover. Cheating of any kind will disqualify your team from the race. Any interference with the other team will find the same result. Each of you will be given five thousand dollars per month from now until the race is completed. This will cover your family's expenses while you train and compete. Each of you will be provided a trainer for the next two months while you prepare for this event. You will be allowed one ten minute phone call per week to your wives during the competition. You will receive instructions periodically on what the next challenge that you face will be. You should prepare yourself for anything and everything. The game begins two months after my funeral. I know that each group does not like the other, which makes this thing much more fun. I love you guys and good luck." And with a grin on his face, that was the end of the tape.

Mr. Craig turned off the television and stood in front of us. The room was still silent, as each of us could not believe what we had just heard. Mr. Craig said "There are a few things that we need to go over. The Ultimate Challenge will begin on April 19th and will conclude when every member of one team crosses the finish line. I will be in charge of any judgments made during the contest. Your instructions will be very clear throughout the challenge. Your safety will be a top priority at all times and we will take all precautions possible to insure your safety. The only information that you will be given about the contest is what you hear today. The Ultimate Challenge will begin and end at Stone Mountain Park. While the contest will be grueling, you will have plenty of food and comfortable accommodations when available. You will be required to give

THE ULTIMATE CHALLENGE

media interviews before and after the challenge. The media will be allowed to monitor your progress during the training period. The Ultimate Challenge will be televised continually on a one hour tape delayed basis. That way we can edit anything that is inappropriate for family viewing. We want you to be yourself and realize that nothing will be aired that is not appropriate."

"Last, I need to inform you that several corporations will be helping to finance The Ultimate Challenge. Reebok and Nike will provide all of your clothing and shoes. Hilton brand hotels will provide your lodging when a hotel stay is applicable. Gatorade and Dasani water will provide you with drinks whenever you need them. You will not be required to endorse these products, just use them during the challenge."

"Gentlemen, I will close by saying that you are about to become instant celebrities. The Expedition Channel will be launching with your race and millions of dollars have been spent on media buys to advertise it. Mr. Simmons wants to protect you by offering my services for free legal counsel after the contest and Fidelity Investments will offer free financial advice after the challenge. I will give you your first five thousand dollar check now. After having a couple of days to tend to personal matters, I will contact each of you with instructions and I will answer any questions that you may have. I will be available to you twenty four hours per day until this contest is over. That is all that I have for you, I'm sure that you need to meet with your families so have a good day and good luck."

We shook hands with Mr. Craig and our new opponents and left the building in a state of numbness. Over the course of the past hour, each of our lives had changed forever. We were just given an opportunity that no one in the world has ever gotten. As we walked back to the car my friends and I just looked at each other, speechless.

We got into the car and Eric's football coach mentality took over. He started yelling and high-fiving everybody. "Thank you Jesus. Thank you Jesus" he said. He then started singing at the top of his voice "We're going to win the money.

We're going to win the money." You have to understand Eric's exuberance. This guy could spend his money as fast as he got it. Back in college, he thought that Bojangles chicken biscuits were his God given right. If their stock price spiked during his four years of college, it was because of him. If I had a dollar for every time that he complained about not having money in college, I would already be a rich man. I turned to Drew and said "This is one get rich quick scheme that might actually work." Drew just had a grin on his face from ear to ear. Jason was the quiet one. He looked straight ahead and with no expression in his voice just said "Oh my God."

After a brief discussion we decided to call our wives and tell them that we could be gone for a couple more hours. We wanted to go somewhere and devise our initial strategy. I called Susan at the hotel and she said that Thomas had just woke up from a nap and they wanted to go shopping anyway. We decided to meet them back at the hotel in three hours. That bought us enough time to go back to the hotel and meet for a while before sharing the news with our wives.

Chapter 3

We went to Drew's room to meet. My leadership skills immediately took over. "I have a few ideas on how we can start this meeting" I said. "First we need to discuss logistics. With an opportunity like this, I am going to resign from my job tomorrow to focus on training for the next two months. What do you think?"

One by one each guy agreed that they would quit their jobs. It was basically a no brainer for even the most conservative person. "Good. That was easy. My next idea is that I think we need to train together and meet daily to discuss what we need to be working on."

Eric spoke up "Drew and I live in Rome so if Jason would agree to move down here from Nashville, then we could make Berry College our training ground. I still work out there several times a month, so I still have contacts. Jason was mulling over this possibility. He loved Nashville but he also didn't want to be difficult. "I'll talk it over with Kim but it does make sense" Jason said.

I wanted to ease Jason's mind. "Jason, you don't have to sell your house. I'm not going to sell mine. I will just bring what we need for two months from Texas and worry about the house later. You can rent an apartment in Rome for two months. You've got five thousand dollars a month to help with expenses." That helped convince Jason.

I needed to get all of my points across. "I have two more things to put on the table for discussion. First, I think that teamwork will be an essential part of winning this thing, so we need to discuss our strengths, weaknesses and personality differences. We have to work on building a team because we will be frustrated with each other at some point."

Drew added "Mark is right. We need to realize what each of us can do in order to maximize our strengths."

Eric jumped in and made my last point "We also need a leader. It needs to be someone that can think with a clear head and make decisions under pressure. I vote for Mark." Jason and Drew agreed, so I was our leader.

"The main thing that I want to do as the leader is keep communication lines open. I think that we need to eat the same, train the same and start building unity. We don't need someone that is struggling to try to be a hero. We all have to cross that finish line to win the money."

We spent the next hour discussing training, diet and what we needed to prepare for. We decided to eat a balanced diet that was low in sugar and high in protein and carbs. I was the only member of the group with weight to lose. I was about fifteen pounds overweight. I could easily lose that in two months. Eric was in great shape. Being a wrestling coach always kept him fit. Drew ran six miles a week so he was in decent shape. But Jason had made the biggest transformation from our college years. Two years ago he lost thirty pounds by running which he really enjoyed and he had kept the weight off.

Our training regimen was going to include weight training, running, hiking a lot and climbing. Berry College was by far the best place to be because the campus was huge and included a mountain. We figured that the main challenge for us would be to train our bodies to cover long distances on foot.

THE ULTIMATE CHALLENGE

The women would be back soon so we made some final plans. We would all leave tomorrow morning with plans to meet in Rome to begin training on Wednesday morning. That gave us three days to take care of personal matters. We were all still in our dress clothes so we decided to get a shower, change and wait for our wives to return to deliver the good news.

Everyone met in my room to wait for the girls. We could hear them as soon as they opened the car door. When these four women get together they make a lot of noise. As soon as they entered the room they knew something was up because we were all quiet with stupid grins on our faces. "What? What? What?" they all screamed. We all looked at each other before Drew said "Mark, you are the leader you tell them."

This was going to be the most fun that I had all day. "Ladies, please sit down. We have something to tell you." They were all about to ring my neck because they could tell by our expressions that something big was up. "John's will was interesting to say the least. Basically, he is going to leave tens of millions of dollars to either us or his high school friends." I couldn't get another word out of my mouth. All four women went crazy hugging us, jumping up and down and screaming at the top of their lungs. Then one by one they realized that what I said was confusing. My wife raised her hands for silence and once again all eyes were on me. "What does that mean exactly?" she asked. I explained "What it means is that we are going to compete in a race against his high school friends to see which team wins one hundred million dollars. The winners get everything, the losers get nothing."

We spent the next hour explaining all of the details to our wives. They had a lot of questions that we couldn't answer but they all agreed that they would sacrifice whatever was needed to help us win.

The next morning Thomas woke me up bright and early and I told him that we were going to see his grandparents. We were going to leave him with them for a few days and I also needed to tell my boss that I was resigning. It was a really bittersweet moment for me. Worth Sports was based out of my hometown so I always felt a special loyalty when I was working in states that were hundreds of miles away. I personally knew many of the people that were making the products that I sold. When I was on a long drive in the middle of nowhere, I would always remember the people that I knew at the factory whose jobs were dependent upon my production. They were working hard to make the bats and balls that I was selling so I always took my job very seriously.

Tullahoma Tennessee is a small town in middle Tennessee that is very unique in a lot of ways. An Air Force base is located just on the outskirts of the town and always brought families from all around the country to make our city more diverse than most. It has a fine arts center and a center for performing arts, so the small town was a great place to grow up.

Thomas fell asleep around the Tennessee state line and without his interruptions our conversation turned more serious. Susan had resisted the question for a while but finally asked "What would you want to do with all of that money?"

"Good question" I answered. "To be totally honest I haven't even thought about it yet. There are a few obvious things. I would want for us to invest enough of it in safe mutual funds so that we could live in luxury off of the interest for the rest of our lives. I would want you to have anything you wanted, to spoil you rotten. I would also want to put away money for Thomas in a trust fund. But the thing that I would enjoy the most is telling my parents that they could retire. What about you? What would you want? Susan grabbed my hand and said "I want to do all of those things and also pick out several worthy charities to give to.

I couldn't wait to tell my parents about this. I was very close with both of them. As I have grown older and become a parent, I now realize the great sacrifices that they made for me growing up. Their lives became whatever their children were doing. They attended ball games, campouts and whatever else we

THE ULTIMATE CHALLENGE

were involved in. As a kid, I thought that everyone else's family was like ours. I grew up in a middle class family and both parents worked very hard to provide us with whatever we needed. I didn't really appreciate my childhood until I grew older and realized that not every family had the love and attention that I got. My dream for the last ten years has been to be able to provide financially for my family, to take the stress off of their shoulders of having to live month to month. I know that I can't take care of all of their problems, but I have always wanted to be able to allow them the luxury of not having to worry about money.

My parents were cautiously optimistic about The Ultimate Challenge. They were worried about me quitting my job because it was a good one, but they were also realistic enough to see that this was a once in a lifetime opportunity. My boss was not too happy when I broke the news to him. He was just upset that I was leaving immediately with no warning. After thinking about it for a while, he changed his thought process and wished me luck.

Chapter 4

After what felt like an around the world trip to Texas and back, we arrived at Drew's house in Rome, Georgia at 9:00 A.M. Wednesday morning. We were exhausted from the trip but knew that there was a lot of work to be done. Everyone was waiting at Drew's house for our arrival. Eric had found a furnished apartment for both Jason and I. Susan went with Kim to sign the leases and start unpacking in our new homes for the next few months. Drew had talked with Ron Craig to decline our need for a personal trainer. Eric was a fitness fanatic so we decided to train on our own. Mr. Craig informed Drew that we had interviews scheduled with reporters from all of the major networks and of course the Expedition channel.

We decided to go to Berry College to begin our training. Eric had contacted the athletic director at Berry and we had twenty four hour access to all of their facilities. Our former college was in fact the perfect training ground for us. It was the largest college campus in the world. Less than two thousand students attended Berry, so the majority of the land was a combination of farmland and mountains. Berry is one of the most beautiful places that I have ever been. Henry Ford financed the building of a gothic styled complex of buildings that have been used in the filming of several movies. The Ford buildings are used in a variety of ways but I always considered them the most beautiful part of the campus. We would spend the majority of our time on the other side of campus, about a mile away where a weight room and swimming pool are located. We would also use the Win Shape campus. It was located about five miles into the forest away from the main campus. It was located at the foot of a mountain and was beautiful in its own right. It had dormitories, a beautiful chapel, class rooms and a water wheel with hiking trails all around. We would leave from Win Shape to hike in the north Georgia Mountains.

We arrived on campus at 10:30 A.M. We entered the front gates of Berry College, took a left in front of the administration building and drove to our new training facility, slowing several times to allow students to cross the road. Jason rode in the car with me and was surprised to see how young the college students looked. "Man this makes me feel old" he said.

"Yeah, but it brings back a lot of memories."

We passed three sets of red brick classroom buildings, the library that we never spent enough time in and our old dormitories.

"Jason, you look nervous."

"I am nervous" he replied. "This whole thing is nuts. I'm mostly nervous about the reporters."

I knew the reporters would be a problem for Jason. He was extremely intelligent, much smarter than me, but he was a little shy until you really got to know him. He didn't really like to venture out of his comfort zone. In college I used to enjoy embarrassing him. On our very first day at Berry College, I did just that. After everyone was unpacked, the Resident Assistant on our dorm room floor called a meeting to welcome us to Berry. Jason and I were rooming together but had not yet introduced ourselves to anyone. We all met in the hallway outside of our rooms and everyone sat on the floor. There were probably fifty people in attendance. I was in shorts, sitting with my back against the wall. Jason was sitting next to me to my left. As the Resident Assistant paused between sentences, I accidentally let out a huge fart. It sounded like something coming out of a tuba. This thing was loud and unexpected, so there was nothing that I could do to cover it up. After the first blast of laughter from the group, I immediately turned to Jason and said loudly "Man, what did you eat?" Jason was terribly embarrassed. He just put his head down and his face turned as red as a beet. That was funny then but now I had to calm him down.

"Look Jason, you are one of the smartest, well-spoken people that I know, so don't worry about the reporters. I promise you that I will answer most of the questions."

Jason perked up "It's a deal. I would really appreciate it if you would do that."

We pulled into the gym parking lot and Drew opened his trunk. It looked like we had robbed a Reebok store. There were running, walking, cross-training and hiking shoes. The stash also included a ton of performance wear for all temperatures, socks, hats and even gloves. We made our way into a side door of the gym, down a flight of stairs and into the weight room — affectionately known as The Pit. Berry had recently opened a new state of the art fitness facility but we decided to go old school to the gym that we used to go to. It brought back a lot of great memories for me because I worked in The Pit for a summer during college. When we all got down into our old weight room, I decided to start things on a lighter note. "Eric, have you seen Little House on the Prairie lately?" Eric looked at me immediately with fire in his eyes.

"What does that have to do with anything? Drew asked. I looked at Jason and he was already grinning because he knew the story.

"I walked in on Mr. Macho Eric here one morning and he was watching Little House on the Prairie. He was bored and no one was in the weight room that morning, so I didn't think much of it. Then when I took a second look, he was trying to secretly wipe tears out of his eyes."

Jason and Drew were already laughing but poor Eric didn't find it so funny. He just ignored everyone. "Focus everyone. We need to focus" he said while trying not to laugh himself. That was who we were. When we got together, no one was safe from jokes being made about them. None of us hassled anyone else. It was just our way of bonding.

Eric said that on the first day we needed to max out on the bench press. That meant bench pressing as much as we could. I was terrible at the bench press because of a dislocated shoulder in high school. My doctor told me then to never go over two hundred pounds because the shoulder repair could fail.

The Pit was just as we had left it. It was painted in blue and white with mirrors on the wall to make it look bigger than it really was. The free weights were on the left with the machine weights, tread mills and stair masters to the right. I was the first person on the bench press. I made it to two hundred pounds and decided not to press my luck. I was happy with two hundred pounds. Jason threw up 225, Drew made it to 215 then Eric stepped up and lifted 275. Eric started strutting around the room with his arms and chest puffed out so I thought I would knock him off his high horse.

"I could bench 275 too if all I had to do was lift the bar six inches to have my arms fully extended."

"Shut up Holland" Eric snapped while proudly admiring his shoulders in the mirror.

Eric's inferiority complex is definitely his height. If you want to push his buttons all you have to do is say something about his height. We had tons of nicknames for him including Tattoo, shrimp, half pint and Smurf. We always kidded him in good fun. He is actually one of the most loyal friends that anyone could ever have. He was the most sentimental guy in our group and he was always good at keeping in touch. So behind his cocky demeanor and short temper, he is actually a great guy.

We lifted weights for about an hour working all of the muscle groups in the upper body. We then decided to go for a jog. We knew of a three mile route that

THE ULTIMATE CHALLENGE

would take us by the men's dormitories, behind a church then up to the beautiful Ford buildings before taking a straight shot back to the gym. This was going to be interesting but we agreed to take it slow. We started out with everyone talking and kidding around. After about a mile, the talking stopped and I was really starting to sweat. My legs were fine but my lungs were not. Breathing is tough when you are running and out of shape. I made it to the two and a half mile mark before I had to start walking. I was the first one to stop but everyone stopped with me and we were all exhausted except for our runner, Jason.

When we got back to the gym we went for a light lunch at a student center that had several eating options. We decided to take a bicycle ride after lunch before our 3:30 interview. Eric had borrowed four mountain bikes from friends so we mapped out a twelve mile trip, which took us to the mountain campus and water wheel then back.

The bicycle ride was rough on my legs. On the way back from the waterwheel I wasn't sure if I was going to make it. Eric set a fairly swift pace and we all stayed with him. I enjoyed the beautiful scenery as the beauty of spring was all around us. As we pulled into the gym parking lot, we were all completely spent. I felt like I had run a marathon. We parked and locked our bikes then made our way to the men's dressing rooms. I laid flat on a bench for thirty minutes trying to catch my breath. Taking my shoes off was the best feeling of all because my feet were tingling with the delight of the day's exercise being over. Jason and Drew did the same.

"Don't tell me you're tired!" Eric said with a grin on his face. Everyone just ignored his comment. After most of my sweat had dried I decided to peel my clothes off and take a shower before facing the media. When I stood up, my legs almost didn't hold me up. It felt like two twenty pound weights had been inserted into my calf muscles. Eric was leaving the shower as I entered. He looked at my gut and said "Mark, you have got some work to do."

"If we keep doing what we did today, this gut will be gone in a month."

Chapter 5

Mr. Craig had arranged our interview to be held outside of the Ford buildings. We drove up twenty minutes early not knowing what to expect. Mr. Craig had driven up from Atlanta to coordinate the first interview session. We greeted everyone and sat down in the four chairs provided for us and immediately started fielding questions. We were asked to introduce ourselves and tell a little bit about our background. Then the questions began.

The reporter from CNN started "How does it feel to be competing in a race for one hundred million dollars?"

Drew spoke up "It feels great. Nothing like this has ever been done before."

Another reporter jumped in "How do you prepare for an event like this?"

Eric handled this question "We plan to train hard every day. We are going to eat a balanced diet and meet daily to discuss what challenges we may be facing."

The same reporter asked a follow up question "Is it true that you guys have refused the services of a trainer?"

I intended to answer the difficult questions "Yes that is true. Eric is a fitness fanatic and also a high school wrestling coach which I believe is the most physically demanding sport that you can participate in."

A third reporter asked "How do you feel about your competitors and what do you think are your chances of winning?"

I answered this question also "To be honest with you we don't really know anything about them and don't care to. They appear to be decent athletes but other than that, your guess is as good as mine. And to answer your second question, we are here to win and plan on doing so."

The questions continued for thirty more minutes with a grand total of two minutes actually being aired on television. After the interview we all felt that it went pretty well. We wanted to seem confident but not cocky. We met that night for dinner at Drew's house. Thomas entertained everyone with the animal noises that he had learned how to make. Our moods were good but we were all tired. Dinner consisted of steamed vegetables and chicken with fruit for dessert. I ate a banana to try to keep from getting leg cramps in the middle of the night.

After dinner we went home to our new apartment. It was nice but small. Thomas had his own room but he would be sleeping in a pack and play for a few months. I was asleep by 8:45, very early for a night person. I slept like a log until 2:30 A.M. when a calf cramp woke me up. A leg cramp is a terrible way to wake up. It felt like there was a huge knot in my calf. Every single time that I wake up with a leg cramp I can never remember if you are supposed to bring your foot forward or away from your body so I did both while rubbing my calf and pleading with God to let it stop.

"What's wrong, sweetie?" Susan asked after being awoken from a dead sleep.

"Calf cramp!" I moaned as I rocked back and forth.

Susan started rubbing my calf and two minutes later I was fine. She leaned over, kissed me on the cheek, and said "I am so proud of you." She then turned over and was sound asleep when her head hit the pillow.

THE ULTIMATE CHALLENGE

Day two of training started slowly. The minute that I rolled out of the bed I knew that this day would not be easy. My body felt like it had been hit by a train. After a couple of minutes of self-encouragement, I convinced my legs that they could work. Susan made me a breakfast of wheat toast and fruit. I ate it while pretending that it was biscuits and gravy with eggs and sausage.

I arrived at Berry around 8:30 to meet the rest of the guys. We were all walking more like senior citizens than thirty year olds. Eric promised us that if we started our day out with a swim, it would help loosen our muscles so we did what he said. Adjacent to The Pit was an Olympic sized swimming pool. We agreed that twelve laps each would be a good goal for today. On about the fourth lap, my muscles did start to feel better.

After our swim we drove to the Win Shape campus to try out the rock climbing wall. Among the goodies from Reebok was four pair of shoes that were designed specifically for rock climbing. Climbing the wall was easier than we thought. After a few failed attempts, I learned to focus on my next step rather than worrying about getting to the top. It was definitely a mind over matter thing. Rock climbing was the fun part of our day. We ate an early lunch at 11:00 and then decided to hike up Mount Berry. We knew that walking or hiking over long distances was an essential part of our training. On the top of Mount Berry was a house called the House of Dreams. There was a dirt road that took you there. The road was five miles each way and the slope was pretty steep. After about a mile of hiking up the road I was really feeling a burn in my thighs. It wasn't unbearable but it was no walk in the park either. Jason led the way and set a steady pace.

"How are you guys doing?" I asked.

"No sweat" Eric replied.

"I feel pretty good" Drew said.

Jason just kept walking. We were all pretty tired when we reached the House of Dreams but the view was amazing. You could see for miles. The house was built for the founder of the college, Martha Berry. No one else was up there so we decided to sit and talk for a while.

"One thing that I wanted to talk about is what special skills each of us have."

"I'm pretty good with engines" Drew said.

"That is good because the rest of us are mechanical idiots. Have you ever worked on boat engines?"

"I have worked on a couple of them but I will have my father in law give me a refresher course."

"I am good at reading maps" I said.

"That's good because I get lost in my own neighborhood" Jason replied.

After half an hour of recuperation we started the hike back. The hike down the mountain was much easier and when we reached the bottom we called it a day.

After one week of intense training I had lost five pounds. This was the hardest that I had ever pushed myself and the soreness was starting to get better. Everyone in the group felt good. We could all run three miles and our ten mile hikes were getting easier. On the third day of week two we decided to challenge ourselves a little more. There was a fifteen mile trail that was really a logging road that ran throughout the forest. It started at the Win Shape campus and ended on a highway that was about half a mile from the main entrance of the college. The road was wide enough so that we could all walk side by side. We made very good time while still taking a water break every three miles. With

THE ULTIMATE CHALLENGE

about a mile and a half to go we picked up the pace, ready to finish our hike. Eric had pulled about ten feet ahead of the rest of us. I had my head up trying to see the highway when out of the corner of my eye I saw Eric jump and heard him scream at the same time.

"Snake! Snake!" he yelled at the top of his lungs.

When Eric landed he was about four feet from the snake. The rest of us were about six feet away from the snake on the opposite side that Eric was on. I could tell right away that we were dealing with a copperhead. It appeared to be about four feet long but it was curled up ready to strike with its eyes directly on Eric. I could feel my heart pounding against my chest. We were all frozen, unsure of what the next move should be.

After taking a few seconds to gain my composure I said "Eric, don't make any sudden movements. Slowly back away and keep your eyes on the snake. The snake was close enough to Eric to bite him if it wanted to. Eric backed away slowly, one labored step at a time. The snake still had not seen us as Eric was walking backwards toward the highway. Eric took eight steps back without any movement from the snake. Then Drew made a sudden move to the left as he had lost his balance. The snake sensed his movement and started turning its body slithering directly toward us. We all jumped back quickly, ready to run in the direction from which we had come. As we jumped back the snake saw an opening and slithered into the bushes on the side of the road.

We all started walking again, happy to be alive. Jason and I looked at each other three times walking a little faster with each glance. We then both took off in a full run for half a mile not caring if our friends thought we were wimps or not. We stopped and waited for our friends to catch up. We both were bent over with our hands on our knees, winded from the sprint.

"I would rather face a hungry lion than a poisonous snake" I said to Jason between gasps.

Jason answered "That scared the living crap out of me."

We both caught our breath by the time that Eric and Drew caught up with us. They were both laughing.

"Would you ladies like to join us for dinner?" Eric sarcastically said.

The quick witted Jason jumped right back on him "I don't know why you're laughing at us, at least we didn't cry at Little House on the Prairie!"

Eric was fuming "I almost get bit by a poisonous snake and all you sons of bitches can do is laugh. You can all kiss my hairy butt. If you tell one person that I teared up watching that show, I will personally beat the crap out of you." We all knew that when Eric went on a yelling spree that it was time to lay off. We all tried to suppress our laughter but it was almost impossible. It was just like when something really funny happens in church. You want to laugh but you try with all of you might to hold it in. I did fine until we got back to our cars. We were all about to get in our cars when I let out a half snort, half snot belly laugh that I tried to pass off as a cough. That made Jason and Drew bust out laughing. Eric looked at us with a look that could kill and said "To hell with all of you. I am going home."

Chapter 6

After a month of training I could see a noticeable difference in my body. I had lost twelve pounds, my chest went from flabby to hard and my legs felt like I could run forever. Our runs were up to five miles each and our hikes were fifteen miles long. We ran four times a week and hiked the other three. Training was getting old but the prize was much too great to complain. After a day of working out, I arrived home around 5:00 to find Susan cooking dinner. I had to use the restroom, so I took my latest Sports Illustrated to the bathroom, also known as my office.

After settling in to learn about the week in sports, I could hear Thomas crying. It was his hurt cry. He had about four different cries but it was easy to tell when something was really wrong. I got off of the toilet and ran into the living room. Before I could say anything Susan said "I gave him peanut butter on a cracker and now his eyes are swelling up."

"We are going to the emergency room right now!" I screamed with fear in my voice.

Luckily Floyd County medical center was only three miles away so we grabbed Thomas and left immediately. It was pouring rain outside, raining so hard that it was difficult to see to drive. The traffic was heavy but I drove like a maniac. I had my emergency lights flashing and we ran every red light, slowing down to stop traffic before entering each intersection.

"How is his breathing?" I asked.

"It's fine. Just calm down." Susan replied.

"My cousin David is deathly allergic to peanuts and if you are allergic to it your tongue and throat swell when you eat it" I said with alarm.

"He is doing fine, Mark" Susan answered.

I checked his breathing every thirty seconds, with the alarm in my voice scaring Thomas and Susan even more than they already were.

We pulled into the hospital and I dropped them off at the Emergency entrance. Thomas' eyes were very swollen. The lady in admitting led us straight into her office but she still had to take down some information. After a series of basic questions she still had to weigh him and take his vital signs. As she was fumbling around with equipment that wasn't working properly, Thomas started having trouble breathing. She immediately dropped what she had and took us back to the doctors and nurses. Susan overheard her say to one of the nurses "this baby has had an allergic reaction to peanut butter, he is having trouble breathing and I think he could go into cardiac arrest." It was then that Susan realized that we were in real trouble.

The nurses took him immediately but allowed Susan to continue holding him to try to keep him calm. His cry was scary. There was a sound of absolute terror in his cry. Susan remained outwardly calm but I was pacing back and forth frantically in the room. By this time Thomas' right eye was swollen completely shut. You could not even recognize him. The child looked as though he had been beaten. His entire face was swollen. His cheeks and eyes looked like air had been blown into them. He was crying inconsolably. Susan and I glanced at each other and the look in her eyes was one that I had never seen. We were absolutely at the mercy of these doctors and nurses. There was nothing that we could do to help our son except pray. Seconds seemed like hours and in my entire life I had never

THE ULTIMATE CHALLENGE

had this emotion, complete and total fear. My body was numb and my mind was racing so fast that I could not develop one clear thought. I prayed as never before, wanting to see a needle in my son's arm.

I fought off the desire to scream at the nurses to put an IV in. After a few minutes, which seemed like days, they gave Thomas an IV that injected steroids into his bloodstream that counteracted the allergic reaction. Within minutes his breathing improved. Slowly the swelling went down and we could see that he would be okay. After all of the nurses left the room, Susan began to cry tears of guilt saying that this was her fault. I comforted her and insured her that nothing was her fault. I also felt very guilty for not remembering to call an ambulance. They would have had a shot of adrenaline that would have done the trick. We held our son thanking God that he was going to be fine. Thomas finally started to become himself again, getting into all of the medical equipment and saying my name "Da Da."

We returned home after having gone through the scariest day of our lives. Every breath that Thomas took was a sigh of relief. I loved my son and wife more than anything in the world and no amount of money could make me happier than they did. I laid in bed that night unable to sleep, quietly checking on Thomas every hour. I cried that night for the first time in years.

I woke up the next morning with a new perspective on life. I would be unable to put into words what happened the night before. I just knew that I would stop sweating the small stuff and enjoy every day for what it is.

I arrived at Berry around 8:30. Ron Craig had driven up from Atlanta to meet with us. There was one month until The Ultimate Challenge and we couldn't wait for it to get here. Mr. Craig met us at The Pit in his usual three piece suit.

"Hello gentlemen. How are you?" he asked. "I want to check on you guys this morning and go over a few details. The media coverage will gradually increase over the next month."

We had given weekly interviews up to this point with a few camera crews covering some of our workouts. Mr. Craig continued "I have some exciting news. We will be taking you to Atlanta in two weeks to tape a segment that will be aired on the Expedition Channel. It will be the first very large media buy on all of the major networks to promote the show. We will have you there and back in about five hours. We are going to put you in a private plane so that traffic doesn't slow you down. Your competitors will also be interviewed the same day and we will be airing both interviews on the same night back to back. There is no need to be nervous, just be yourselves."

Our meeting lasted about thirty minutes. Susan was a big fan of reality television shows so she would be psyched about watching the interviews. After Mr. Craig left we talked for a while about how big this thing was getting and then we went back to work.

In week five, I achieved two personal milestones. First, I bench pressed two hundred forty pounds which was a new personal record. My other milestone was that I finally overcame the hump of running being work and it started to be fun. I think that I finally achieved what runners call a "runners high." It was about four miles into our daily run and my legs and lungs started to feel great. It felt as though I could run forever. I was Superman but instead of saving the world, I was just running down the street.

We all felt strong. You could tell that the biggest transformation was Jason. He looked and felt like he could do anything. Jason was noticing changes in his muscle structure and he loved it. His energy level rose to a height that I had never seen in him.

Eric told us that over the last ten days of our training that we should continue to work out but also cut back a little to conserve energy and avoid injury. We had been lucky so far because other than a few blisters on our hands and feet, we had been relatively injury free. Eric deserved the credit for this because before we did anything he led us through stretching exercises. He explained to

THE ULTIMATE CHALLENGE

us that flexibility was just as important as strength. My flexibility was so much better than when we started. I went from barely being able to bend over to feeling like Stretch Armstrong.

My brother Keith told us what to possibly expect in the challenges that we could face. He was a thrill fanatic and had tried just about everything at least once. He thought that the challenges might include hiking, biking, running, rock climbing and white water rafting. The truth was that we had no idea what to expect. John Simmons was a really creative guy with a brilliant flare for dramatics. Our friend was gone but still very much alive in our minds.

Our upcoming interview would be the longest segment so far. The Expedition Channel was preparing an hour long show about our two months of training that would air the following night and the night before The Ultimate Challenge began.

Thomas recovered quickly from his peanut butter allergic reaction. We took him the next week to an allergist who supplied us with an Epi-pen. Basically, it is a shot that can be injected into his leg if he has another reaction. The doctor explained that this is something that he will probably deal with for the rest of his life. At least we had a solution if it ever happened again.

Susan was getting accustomed to our new life. She quickly became good friends with my friend's wives and they all spent a lot of time together. We were all trying to be patient while anticipating the big event. My new and improved body also changed Susan's outlook on other things. I tried to save just a little bit of energy every evening for late night festivities. If I had known that working out would have had this effect, I would have been in shape years ago.

Chapter 7

April 6th – Thirteen days until The Ultimate Challenge

Our trip for the interview in Atlanta was fantastic. The Expedition Channel chartered a private jet to take us on the short flight to Stone Mountain where the interview would take place. It was my first trip on a chartered plane. There was no security line, we just drove up to the hangar and hopped on the plane. You could get used to the curbside service very easily.

Drew's house was the site of our watching party. My parents came down from Tennessee and with family members and friends included there were thirty eight people present to watch our interview. Luckily, we had already seen television clips of ourselves over the past month and a half so we knew what to expect. I was shocked at how strong my southern accent was on television. You don't really realize what you sound or look like on television until you watch it yourself. I did look much better now than when we did our first interview. The intense training and weight loss did wonders for my appearance.

Before our fifteen minute segment on the Expedition channel, we planned to watch our competitors whose interview would air before ours. The reality of this event was starting to hit everyone now. All of the training, all of the hiking and running in relative solitude was about to be over. The living room in Drew's house was bustling with nervous excitement.

After a ten minute introduction going over the contest details, the host of the show said "It is now time to welcome our first guests who in two weeks will be competing in The Ultimate Challenge which is a race for one hundred million dollars. Please welcome Ronnie, Larry, Doug and Phil. There was a live studio audience that applauded as our opponents greeted the host. They all wore dark blue Wrangler jeans, cowboy boots and belt buckles about the size of your hand.

"Hello everyone" said the host, a dark haired and handsome young man that the Expedition channel had plucked from another network. "The Ultimate Challenge is amazing. I can't even fathom competing in a race for one hundred million dollars. How does it feel?"

"It feels good" Ronnie answered. He was their leader and always had been since we first met them in college. He was stocky with dark balding hair that was cut very short.

"What do you do to get ready for something like this?" the host asked.

Ronnie answered "We started out working with a personal trainer but we didn't like him much so now we are just working out on our own."

The host continued "You guys look like cowboys. Do you work on a ranch?"

Phil jumped in. He was very skinny with long blond hair that was tied in a pony-tail. "No. This is just how real men dress in the south."

His next question was when the interview took a turn for the worse. "Do you guys know anything about your competition?"

Doug chimed in. Doug was a little overweight but had lost about twenty pounds over the last month and a half. "They look like a bunch of little fairies to me."

THE ULTIMATE CHALLENGE

The host looked straight into the camera, unsure of how to proceed. "You are Doug, correct?"

"Yes sir."

"Do you want to elaborate on what you mean exactly by saying they look like fairies?"

"What I mean is that they look like weak little punks to me. They look like they have never done an honest day's work in their life. Like they were born with a gold spoon in their mouth."

"Do you mean a silver spoon?" the host asked while trying to get a reaction.

"Gold spoon, silver spoon, I really don't care what the saying is. Wimps is a good word for them. They look like wimps to me."

"Well, let's discuss something else" the host said. "If you guys win, what do you plan on doing with the money?"

Larry jumped in with "I want to open my own pool hall. It would have plenty of space and a great bar serving every kind of beer and whiskey known to man. It would have a jukebox filled with old country music and a dance floor." Larry was the quiet one of the group. He had red hair and a big tattoo of an eagle on his forearm with the name of his wife written below it."

"A pool hall" the host repeated. "That's nice Larry."

"What about you Doug?"

"I'm going to buy me three liquor stores and sell booze to everybody in the county."

CHARLES LUNA

Phil finished off with "I'm not going to do anything with my money except quit working and become a professional beer drinker."

The look of surprise on the hosts face was evident. "Well it is good to hear that you all have such lofty expectations." This got a generous laugh from the audience. "I wish you all the best of luck." He then turned to the camera and said "The Ultimate Challenge will be aired twenty four hours per day on the Expedition Channel. We will be right back with the other team."

The segment was obviously cut short. These guys should have been on Jerry Springer but they made an impression. I was embarrassed for them. We knew that John grew up in a rural area but we didn't know how rural until we got a better look at those guys. We knew that they were rough when we met them at our house in college but we figured that they had matured a little since then. Everyone in the house got a few good laughs.

I looked at my teammates and said "That was ridiculous. We can't take these guys for granted. If we were matching wits it would be easy but you don't have be polished to be good at physical challenges." There was a growing dislike for our competitors around the room. The competition had just become personal, which is exactly what John Simmons knew would happen. He knew that the rivalry would only help the drama surrounding the greatest idea of his life.

We visited for the next five minutes waiting for our longest and most watched interview yet. The atmosphere was festive and a great time to enjoy family and friends. We had the recorder set, ready to tape this once in a lifetime event. As 8:00 neared we all gathered around Drew's wide screen television and the room became silent.

The opening song began and I had butterflies in my stomach. The entire country was tuning in for this one. The host came out to a resounding applause

THE ULTIMATE CHALLENGE

and when it finally tapered off he started. "Thank you everybody. In the previous hour, you all met John Simmons high school friends that will be participating in The Ultimate Challenge. In a moment we will meet the other team, his four college housemates. To remind everyone watching, these two teams will square off in a race to determine which team will win one hundred million dollars. For those of you like me that dream of your wildest fantasies coming true, you are about to meet four men that have that opportunity. When we come back from this commercial break, we will be joined by Team Reebok."

"Our next guests are two weeks away from competing for an amount of money they never dreamed was possible. Let's welcome Jason, Mark, Eric and Drew to the show." This was our cue. We left the small holding room and entered through a side door. The crowd was applauding as we made our way to the set. This was very different than being interviewed by a few reporters. This was live and in front of a studio audience. This was the first live audience that we have experienced with the exception of a few college students at Berry that were just passing time between classes. We all took our seats near the commentator.

"Welcome everybody."

"Thank you for having us" Drew responded.

"So how did it happen? Are you just sitting on your couch one day and get a phone call from an old friend that wants you to race for a bunch of money?"

I chimed in "It's actually a really sad story. A guy by the name of John Simmons was a college house-mate of ours. He was a self-made billionaire with no wife or siblings. His parents were dead. Unfortunately he found out that he had terminal brain cancer with only a few months to live. So he spent the last two months of his life inventing The Ultimate Challenge. It is a race between us and four of his high school friends with the winner walking away with one hundred million dollars. After his funeral we watched a video will that he had made and that is how we found out about it."

"Wow" the host said acting surprised when in reality he knew the entire story. "So you guys must have mixed emotions about this."

"Yes we do" Eric answered. "It is hard to believe that John is gone, but he loved adventure, he loved competing and he loved planning big events."

"I know that the event is called The Ultimate Challenge. Exactly what challenges are you guys going to face?"

Drew spoke up. "Good question. That is what makes the whole thing so intriguing. We really have no idea what the challenges will be. All that we were told was to prepare for anything and everything and that we would be traveling all over the country. We know that it begins and ends at Stone Mountain, Georgia and that is it."

The host responded "So really, you are going into this high stakes race with no idea of what you have to do to win."

"Exactly" Drew said. "I think that is one of the reasons that The Ultimate Challenge is starting to be hyped as much as it is. The viewers can literally live this race with us. We won't know anything that the people at home watching don't know. After we complete one challenge then we will find out what the next challenge will be. It is really a work of genius."

The host continued "My guess is that with the success of reality television, John Simmons decided that this format might be a success."

"That is a tough question to answer" Jason said. "A brand new channel, The Expedition Channel has a lot to lose or gain. But the creator of the show is dead, so he probably did not care if it was a success or not. I'm sure that with the amount of money at stake that this type of show will never be done again to this degree. How many times is a man as wealthy as John Simmons going to pass away and let his friends battle it out for his fortune? I would guess never."

THE ULTIMATE CHALLENGE

The host's next question was "How does it feel going from an ordinary life to being thrown into the limelight with a chance to win a fortune?"

Jason, more comfortable now added "It is literally like living in a dream. The entire thing is really mind blowing. But we all know that one reason John Simmons came up with this game is that at the end of his life, he realized that money can't buy happiness. He did know that great friends who always stand by each other definitely does bring you happiness. In our case, we have really lost touch with each other. We all have families and most of us have moved away. So this is his way to kind of teach us a lesson. So it's not all about the money."

"I am guessing that the money is nice though?"

"Oh yeah. Definitely."

The host looked at me. "Mark, I understand that you have lost quite a bit of weight while you guys have been training?"

"Yes I have. So far, I have lost twenty pounds." The crowd applauded for me.

"That is great" the host said enthusiastically. "Well your friends are so proud of your progress that they wanted to share it with the world!" The host then turned around and behind us was my worst nightmare. I knew that I was in trouble before I looked behind me because Eric was laughing so hard that he fell out of his chair. I turned to my right, dreading what I was about to see.

"This is the before picture" the host said with an emphasis on the word before. The crowd laughed as I turned a dark shade of red.

There it was, on national television, a picture of me with my shirt off taken two months ago. My gut was hanging down and it looked like a beach ball that was attached to my body. My love handles stuck out so far that my torso looked more like a pear than a person. And my flabby boobs could have filled a good sized bra. My cheeks were so fat that it looked like I had just had my wisdom teeth pulled and my double chin hung low, flapping in the breeze.

Susan had taken the picture just kidding around one day. I got mad at her then and she promised me that she would never show it to anyone. I was going to get her for this.

My friends were as red as I was. They were not embarrassed at all, they were laughing their butts off. The host then finally let me off the hook.

"And here is the after picture" he said. Next to my old body, a picture of my new body came up. It was really quite a transformation. I even got a few whistles from the women in the audience.

The damage was done. My friends had gotten me. That is the way that it was with us. No holds barred. If you can't take a beating then you can't be our friend. One thing that I did know was that I would probably never be able to top this. I did want to scare Eric though because I was sure that it was his idea in the first place. As the laughter continued, I leaned over to him and whispered "See Little House on the Prairie lately?" A look of panic overcame him as he sternly whispered back "I swear to God Holland, if you say one word!" I then turned away having taken a little pleasure from this awful moment. No one knew it, but I had gotten him back. I scared him to death. One down, two to go.

The host didn't want to embarrass me any more so he changed the subject. "We have time for one last question. If you win, what do you each plan to do with the money?"

After what my friends had put me through, I deserved to answer the question. "Well, we each have our dreams and goals, but there are a couple of things that I have in mind. One is to help raise money to cure cancer. It is so crazy that John was stricken with deadly brain cancer at such an early age. And children that are diagnosed is even more emotional for me. So I know that I will donate

THE ULTIMATE CHALLENGE

a large portion to the American Cancer Society earmarked for research for a cure. It is a horrible disease. Cancer really doesn't care how wealthy you are, how old you are, what color your skin is or if you are a man or woman. It is equally terrible to everyone. My other big donation will be to help dig water wells in several countries in the Sahara desert. I watched a documentary about it and it really touched me. The water is already there. They just need a way to access it because it is deep below the ground."

The host thanked us and said "The Ultimate Challenge will be airing on the Expedition channel beginning on April 19th. Thanks guys."

We purposely kept our segment of the show a secret to our families so that we could relive the event with them. Everyone got plenty of laughs at my expense and the entire afternoon was fun for everyone. I didn't chastise Susan about the picture. Instead I hugged her and Thomas more than usual because I knew that very soon I would not be able to do that.

Chapter 8

April 17, 2 days until The Ultimate Challenge

After seven weeks of training and dozens of interviews, we were all eager for the big day to arrive. I was in the best shape of my life and felt prepared for anything that we might face. We toned down our training, just trying to maintain and not get injured. Time slowed to a crawl and we were playing a waiting game. We had a lunch meeting with Mr. Craig to go over last minute details.

"So are you ready?" he asked us all with enthusiasm.

We all nodded yes. "There are a few things that we need to go over. Tomorrow we have rooms for each of you and your families at the Marriot inside of Stone Mountain Park. That way you will not have to worry about the crowds the next morning. The Ultimate Challenge will begin at 10:00 A.M. Prior to the start of the race, we will be introducing each of you. The race will begin immediately after with a five mile race around Stone Mountain. Your route will be taped off for the entire five miles. We are expecting thousands of spectators and dozens of camera crews. You will not be required to give interviews on the day of the race. We will need you to be ready one hour prior to the introductions. We are going to take some pictures and go over any last minute details. I also want you to meet the camera crew from the Expedition channel that will be with you during the first leg of the race. We are going to supply you with one cell phone for calls to your family and you will have a direct line to me in case of questions or an emergency. We will have security in place at Stone Mountain to prevent anyone from interrupting you. I am going to give you directions to the hotel and we will keep the media away from you tomorrow night so that you can each have a quiet evening with your families. Do you guys have any questions?"

We had tons of questions but none that Ron could answer so we ordered our lunch and talked about Major League baseball for an hour.

I arrived home at 3:30 so that I could spend as much time as possible with Susan and Thomas. To my delight, Thomas wanted to play ball as soon as I arrived. He was learning how to catch but he didn't understand the concept of throwing the ball back to me. He just loved to throw the ball and run after it himself. Susan was glad to see me.

"I am really going to miss you two."

"We will miss you too, the only difference is that we can watch you anytime that we want. So when Thomas asks for you, I will just show him the television."

"I want to tell you that I really appreciate how great you have been. It is really going to be hard to take care of him all day every day."

Susan approached and wrapped her arms around me "It will all be worth it if you win."

"You are not kidding!" I said. "I can't even fathom that much money. Just think, we will never have to worry about mortgage payments, car payments and we can stop clipping coupons. No more arguments about spending. It would be an absolute dream."

Susan smiled "We could design our dream home and I could buy a Porsche 911."

THE ULTIMATE CHALLENGE

"And I could buy an Audi sports car along with a big F250 to drive on our huge farm. We could build an indoor basketball court, a hitting facility with a state of the art pitching machine. We could get a golf simulator and play every famous course in the world. We could also have an indoor movie theater with surround sound. One of my customers in Houston sells them. You push a button and the curtains opens to a movie screen."

Susan laughed "So you have been dreaming about this after all. Do you realize that this whole time you have not told me one thing that you would want to get if we win?"

"I know" I answered. "I guess that it is all becoming real now since we are only two days away. What would you want?" I asked.

"I want a big house with large spacious rooms, a huge kitchen with two ovens, customized cabinets and all stainless steel appliances. And a built in stereo system that plays throughout the house. I would want the back of the house to be all windows overlooking a swimming pool with a built in waterfall and mountains in the distance behind our farm. And a walk-in closet as big as a bedroom to store all of my clothes. I would want our bedroom to have a sitting area and our bathroom would have his and her showers with a Jacuzzi tub in the middle.

I jumped into her dream. "I would want an octagon shaped office at the top of the house with windows on all sides overlooking our estate. Can you believe that I just said estate?"

Susan continued as her beautiful blue eyes sparkled "I would want a huge dining room that had a big long table, and soft leather couches in all of our living rooms. And skylights, lots of skylights throughout the house."

We had finally done it. We had gone two months without talking about our plans, afraid that if we did, we would immediately wake up from a dream. But we had both been dreaming, each secretly planning the exact same home. One that we had discussed in prior years but knew that we would never build. Now it was at our finger tips.

"Susan, I don't know if we will win or lose but I am going to try my hardest to make your dreams come true. You deserve it. You are great. I don't know what I did to deserve you, but I am already the luckiest man in the world."

Susan put her arms around me again with tears streaming down her face. I didn't tell her these things often enough, so when I did the moments were very special.

"I love you. I love you no matter what. The money would be nice, but having you and Thomas already makes me the happiest woman in the world."

Thomas saw that his momma was crying so he started putting his fists in the air with a smile on his face. That was his way of scaring us and he knew that it made us laugh. We picked him up and had a big family hug. He leaned over and put his tiny lips on Susan's cheek and gave her a kiss. I knew that the hardest part of the coming weeks would not be the physical challenges, but being away from my family.

Chapter 9

April 18th One day until The Ultimate Challenge

Susan, Thomas and I arrived at Stone Mountain Park around 3:00. As we rounded the curve that went to our hotel, we saw a scene that can only be described as organized chaos. Dozens of television trucks were parked in the hotel parking lot. We luckily found a place to park because someone was pulling out as we drove up. The field between the hotel and the mountain looked like a circus. Vendor tents were set up in rows selling everything from The Ultimate Challenge t-shirts to glow in the dark headbands. Thousands of people were mulling around on the day before the race. We made it to about thirty yards from the entrance to our hotel lobby when a reporter recognized me. He yelled a question "Mr. Holland, how do you feel today?" as he hurried toward me with a microphone and his cameraman directly behind him rolling tape. The reporter had caught the attention of everyone around and within seconds we were surrounded by what seemed to be hundreds of people. Claustrophobia started to overcome me as everyone pushed forward, each wanting something, whether it was an autograph, a picture or a quote. Thomas began to cry as all of the strangers running towards us had scared him.

"Back away" I screamed. Just give us a little space." Our efforts to push the crowd away were futile. I had Thomas in one hand and had my arm around Susan with the other.

"What do we do?" she asked.

"We need security."

Just after I said that, eight security guards began breaking the crowd up. We were still unable to move and I felt a panic attack coming on. Adrenaline started pumping through my body and I began to sweat profusely. People were yelling in every direction. My legs began to feel weak and I started to get dizzy. I could feel my heart pumping as I tried to maintain some semblance of composure. Susan saw the fear in my eyes and quickly took Thomas from my arms. The people directly around us were trying to help by pushing the crowd away in every direction. Panic had also set in for two women that were near us. They were being pushed in two different directions and they were not happy at all.

After a couple of minutes that seemed like hours, the security guards broke up the crowd and restored order. They formed a circle around my family and led us into the hotel lobby where no one was allowed unless they had a pass.

I made my way directly to a couch in the lobby to regain my composure. After about five minutes of silence and a bottle of water, I no longer had the feeling that I was going to pass out. I took long deep breaths and closed my eyes, not caring what anyone thought that was looking at me. This was something that I could have never prepared for. I was just a regular guy and have never had anyone really pay any attention to me.

As I sat in the lobby of the hotel that overlooked Stone Mountain, I began to realize just how big this thing had gotten. I really couldn't pin point why so many people were interested. I did know that John Simmons had spent a lot of money on publicity. I guess a lot of people just want to live this race vicariously through us. It was a once in a lifetime thing. Susan joined me on the couch in the lobby after giving me some time to catch my breath.

"Are you okay?" she asked.

THE ULTIMATE CHALLENGE

"I'm fine now. How about you?"

"I'm fine. That was a little scary though."

Ron Craig saw us and approached. He was wearing his usual dark three pieced suit, hair perfectly in place and a look at his face like there was not enough time to get everything done.

"Mark, I am so sorry about the crowd. We had no idea that so many people would show up today. Is everyone all right?"

"We are fine. I just want to keep it from happening again. I had no idea that people would get so crazy about this."

"This race is the talk of the country. Everyone is going to be watching. I guess with most news being negative and confrontational, people just want to invest their time into something else."

By the time that we found our room, unpacked and changed the little guy's diaper it was time to go downstairs for the press conference. I met my teammates in the lobby at 4:30.

"You have a 10:00 curfew tonight" Eric said without even a hello.

"You don't have to even worry about that. Who knows where we will be sleeping tomorrow night."

Drew was the most laid back guy in the group. "I am going to enjoy dinner tonight and sleep like a baby then worry about tomorrow when it gets here."

Mr. Craig led us into a cafeteria that had been turned into a make-shift press room. As we entered the room, hundreds of flash bulbs went off. There were probably two hundred reporters waiting for us. The television cameras were already rolling so we had to act normal. We took our seats in four chairs with a banner showing The Ultimate Challenge logo behind it. The logo was four men standing on the top of Stone Mountain with their hands in the air.

Ron Craig began the press conference by saying that it would last for one hour and to please specify which participant each question was intended for. After the short opening, it sounded like a White House press conference, with every reporter demanding that their question be asked first. Most of the questions that were asked had already been asked a dozen times. We were already pros at this and even Jason looked very comfortable sitting there. There were a few unique questions though.

"Are any of you guys worried about people getting too caught up in this and possibly losing their job?" one crazy reporter asked.

Drew answered "I haven't lost any sleep over it. But for everyone watching, please go to work. We will still be on when you get home."

Drew's response received a laugh from the crowd as the dejected reporter lowered his head.

Another reporter asked, "What will you do if you lose?"

Eric jumped in "I guess we will send a resume to the guys that won."

Most of the question were legitimate but we were relieved when the press conference was over. We were all starving and met our wives in the hotel dining room for a private dinner. After we ate our salads Drew stood up and tapped his glass. "I want to make a toast" he said. "For everyone here I want to thank you for working so hard. We have had a tough few weeks of training and a tough few weeks ahead but we have worked really hard and we are ready. To winning." Drew raised his glass and everyone responded in unison. Drew continued to stand. "I have one other announcement to make." Drew paused for a moment as a huge

THE ULTIMATE CHALLENGE

smile slowly appeared on his face. "I have a new motivation to win. My beautiful wife and I are going to have a baby."

We all stood and offered our congratulations and after the dinner, we all retired early to our rooms. Our room overlooked the carving on Stone Mountain and we opened the curtain to watch the nightly laser show and fireworks. The park had made an exception tonight and allowed patrons to camp outside of the hotel and a tent city formed as thousands waited for the race to begin.

We made Thomas a bottle of milk and laid him down in his pack and play. It had always been difficult getting him to sleep when he was in the same room as we were. We laid him down with the bottle, kissed him goodnight and two minutes later he was standing up, just tall enough to see over the top. He was smiling at us and saying "Ma Ma, Da Da" which were his two favorite words. We always ended up turning all of the lights off and going to sleep because that was the only way to calm him down. Tonight was different though, we wanted to watch the Tonight Show monologue to see if Leno was going to mention us. He did not disappoint.

After greeting the audience he jumped right in. "Has everyone heard about this race called The Ultimate Challenge? For those of you who haven't, it is a race where four guys are competing against four other guys for a prize of one hundred million dollars. Can you imagine that?" Both of the teams appeared for an interview on the Expedition Channel. Here is a clip of them answering a question of what they will do with the money if they win."

Our competitors appeared on the screen. "They look like a bunch of fairies to me." The next guy came on "I am going to open me the best pool hall around." The television flashed back to Leno who raised his eyebrows as the audience laughed. Jay then said "Show the other clip." Jason appeared on the screen "It's not all about the money." Leno appeared once again with a sly grin on his face. "So we have the all redneck team playing against the lying fairies. I have already seen that one before, it was called the Presidential election." The crowd roared with laughter and I alm0st choked on the drink of water that I was having. I just hoped that Jason was already asleep.

We quickly turned the lights off so that Thomas would go to sleep. I tossed and turned continually, getting up three times to pee. I drank a lot of water that day so that I wouldn't get dehydrated the next day and it was backfiring on me. If I pee once and don't go to sleep immediately, for some reason my bladder fills again within minutes and it becomes an endlessly frustrating cycle. I finally nodded off around 12:30 A.M. when my water hose finally ran dry and slept soundly for seven hours.

Chapter 10

The big day had finally arrived and Thomas woke me up by petting my arm. "Hey buddy! Good morning" I said and received a big beautiful smile in return. Susan greeted me with a kiss and told me to look outside the window. There were thousands of people already waiting and the race was finally getting started. I took a shower and got ready then met my friends in the lobby for a light breakfast. Eric was ready and waiting for us and already had his game face on. He greeted me with a chest bump and said "Holland, are you ready to do this thing?" showing his football coaching mentality.

I wanted to lighten the mood a bit as Drew and Jason watched. "Not really" I said while shrugging my shoulders. Eric's eyes grew wide with frustration as Jason and Drew had smiles appear on their faces immediately. I quickly shifted gears and walked right in front of my high strung friend and said very loudly "The question is, are you ready!"

"Let's get it on!" he screamed while pushing my shoulders back a little harder than he meant to.

Jason was smiling but he still looked a little embarrassed. He had watched Leno. "Don't even say it" he said. "I know it was bad."

"Don't even worry about it" Susan said. "He took it way out of context."

Drew was excited and ready for the race to get underway. He stood up and started dancing around trying to churn butter in the awkward way that he always tried to dance. His definition of dancing was putting his hands together and continue making a circle while jumping around. Some things never changed. That has been his one and only dance move since our college days. He always was crazy and crazy would keep us going through the next three weeks. "I'm ready" he shouted in a winded voice while continuing his attempt to dance.

"You might want to sit down before you break something" Jason muttered in his monotone voice without looking up from his food.

I loved these guys because when we all got together it was hard to be nervous. We all had very different personalities, but it just worked. Our way of dealing with difficult situations was to make fun of each other and we were all experts at doing it.

After breakfast we made our way to a conference room where a team of workers were prepared to go over any last minute details with us. We were all dressed in blue and bright green Reebok jogging suits with matching shoes to go with it. We knew that our initial run around Stone Mountain would be about five miles and after that, we did not have a clue. We agreed to set an eight minute mile pace regardless of what the rednecks did. We had some pictures taken and met the camera crew that would be joining us throughout the contest.

The Ultimate Challenge staff had built a stage directly in front of the conference room where we would be introduced. The course was already roped off with a red, white and blue flagged rope mapping out our track to keep the crowd back. The crowd was already ten people deep along the path for as far as I could see. We could hear music playing from the loudspeakers on the stage as the seconds ticked off the clock until our great race began.

At 9:15, thirty minutes before our introduction, we said goodbye to our families and they joined the crowd in a special roped off section for them. Our

THE ULTIMATE CHALLENGE

wives were instructed as we were, that during our ten minute phone calls each week, we were not to discuss the race or our competitors in any way. We would not be allowed to view a television at any time to monitor the other team's progress.

Everyone left the room accept for our cameraman. "Well guys, this is it!" I said. "Let's make sure and communicate. If you need to slow down just say it. This race won't be won or lost today."

"Eric will set a steady pace."

Ron Craig entered our room ten minutes prior to the introduction and was accompanied by Chip Carey, voice of the Atlanta Braves, who was going to handle the introductions. It was an honor for me to meet him because as a lifelong baseball fan, I had watched his grandfather, his dad and now him call Major League baseball games.

Mr. Craig then spoke up "You guys know the rules. We will have medical staff nearby whenever it is possible. Mark, here is a cell phone that clips onto your pants. Keep it on at all times. You can have it on ringer or vibration, we just want to be able to track you and keep in touch if something arises. Press 1 and then send if you need me for any reason. After your name is called, just walk onto the stage and wave to the crowd then step to the right side of the stage. We will introduce the other team first. We will refer to them as Team Nike and you will be Team Reebok.

We could hear the crowd getting louder, anticipating the start of the race with the biggest prize in history. John Simmons must have been smiling down on us because it was his race that everyone was cheering for. We each knew that when we returned to Stone Mountain, we would either be rich or jobless. With two minutes until the introduction began, of course I had to pee. I ran to the bathroom with ten times more nervous energy that any ballgame that I had ever played in. I tried peeing fast but there are some things that you just can't control.

I was panicking because I could not change nature's course. I made it back in just in time to hear Chip Carey's voice address the crowd.

Drew looked at me and said "Are you all right?"

"Oh he is fine" Jason said. "He has been this way his entire life. He always had to pee a lot before he pitched. He has done that since Little League."

We made our way to the door and the roar of the crowd was deafening. As the lady that was instructing us cracked the door we could see the back of Chip Carey. We listened as he began the introduction. "And now we are going to meet Team Reebok. First let's meet Eric Jones who is a football and wrestling coach from Rome, Georgia." The crowd roared as Eric made his way onto the stage, waved to the crowd and flexed his biceps before moving to the right of the stage.

Carey continued "Next we are going to meet Drew Norman. Drew is a thirty year old business owner also from Rome, Georgia. As the crowd cheered for Drew, Jason looked at me with his eyes open wide. He was definitely mortified. "Now we are going to meet Jason Mulkey. Jason is a twenty nine year old insurance adjuster from Nashville, Tennessee. I pushed Jason through the door, he quickly waved to the crowd and rushed to the side of the stage and hid behind his friends.

I was last and was determined to enjoy this. "And finally let's welcome Mark Holland. Mark is a thirty year old sales rep from Fort Worth, Texas." As I walked out of the door and onto the stage I raised both hands in the air with my fists clinched. After pausing for a few seconds to let the atmosphere sink in, I ran over and high fived my teammates. There were people for as far as I could see. I felt nervous, confident, elated and scared to death all at the same time. I found my family and tapped my chest three times to Thomas, which was my way of telling him that I loved him. It was our form of sign language. He was too caught up in the excitement to notice but Susan saw me and did it back.

THE ULTIMATE CHALLENGE

We turned around with all eyes on Chip Carey. "And now the moment that we have all been waiting for. Are you ready for The Ultimate Challenge?"

The crowd went crazy as we made our way to the starting line. The course was about twenty feet wide so there was plenty of room for all eight contestants to step up to the line. Carey battled to be heard over the noise of the crowd.

"Gentleman on your mark. Get set."

I clinched my fists in anticipation of the start of the race, while knowing in the back of my mind that it could last for weeks. I stared straight ahead, waiting for the magical word.

"Go!" Carey screamed.

As Chip Carey shouted go, fireworks shot up from the back of the stage, scaring the crap out of everyone. As we started the race, the rednecks sprinted out to an early lead, which we were happy to relinquish. The four of us ran together, side by side, in the middle of the roped off track. We passed tons of people with many trying to get our attention as we passed. We ran straight towards the mountain for one quarter of a mile before the course turned to the right to begin our trek around the mountain. The weather was clear and cool, perfect conditions for the beginning of our race. A cameraman was filming us from the back of a small Ford pick-up so that the nation could watch us run. We set a steady eight minute mile pace and about two and a half miles into our race we easily passed the winded rednecks, who had slowed to a painful jog. They had gotten caught up in the hoopla and were paying for their burst out of the starting blocks. As we started around the mountain, I was completely surprised that the crowd was still ten deep for as far as I could see. They sported The Ultimate Challenge t-shirts, hats and flags. I waved to them occasionally in appreciation for their excitement.

I tried speaking to Eric who was running next to me but could not hear a thing because there was a continuing roar as we passed. So I decided to just enjoy the moment. This was exactly what I had dreamed of as a child. Thousands of people cheering for my team. The only difference was that in my dream, I was pitching in the seventh game of the World Series. I came to the realization my freshman year in college that my dream was never going to happen. Boy was I wrong.

Since the crowd was too loud for me to speak to my teammates, I thought that I would communicate in another way. I was feeling really gassy from last night's dinner and I had been trying very hard to hold it in for about a mile. It became evident from the pains in my stomach that my efforts were futile, so I sped up and pulled in front of my friends. They thought that I was shouldering the responsibility of leading our team to the finish line, but they would soon learn that their assumptions were not the case. After taking about ten strides in front of them, I just couldn't hold it any longer. The first one was small, but I was now an experienced runner with a love of food, so I knew what was about to happen. My butt became a machine gun with a barrage of bullets that would make any unsophisticated man proud. Once it got going I could not make it stop. Everything was completely out of control and I was just an innocent bystander. I let one out with every stride for about twelve strides. They sounded off with perfect unison with my stride, like the beat of a drum. The only way to stop it would be to stop running and I wasn't willing to do that. I seriously could not stop farting. Thank God the crowd was cheering so that no one could hear it. There was a cameraman in a truck filming the entire thing that was only twenty yards ahead. Drew was the first to catch a whiff of the deadly toxin and covered his nose with his shirt. Jason and Eric then caught wind of it and their faces turned very sour.

I was so relieved when the gunfire finally stopped and considered myself lucky that I didn't crap my pants in front of millions of people that could be eating popcorn in front of their televisions. It was a very childish act for me to pull in front of them but I wanted to keep the mood as light as possible to calm any nerves that I or my teammates might have. Being with them made me regress which also made me happy. With the barrage over and my underwear clean, I dropped back even with my friends.

By the time that we reached the four mile mark, we were all really starting to sweat but I was feeling really good. We were rounding the final turn of the mountain, getting ready to head back to where the race had started when two young guys jumped onto the course by ducking under the ropes. At the time, there was about twenty yards between us and the television truck. The guys ran out about ten feet in front of us waving their hands in the air while facing the camera in the truck. Jason saw them but not quickly enough because they came onto the track from the side that he was running on. Jason tripped over one of the young men and he landed hard, face first onto the pavement. The two college aged kids saw what happened and disappeared quickly into the crowd. We stopped immediately and turned to our fallen friend who was laying on the ground, holding his knee and writhing in pain.

"Are you okay?" I asked.

"I think so. Just give me a minute" he responded in a strange voice.

"Take your time" Drew said. "We are in no hurry."

Jason moved to a sitting position. His arms and face were bloody. His right knee had taken the majority of the blow and blood was streaming from it. Small pieces of pavement were embedded in his knee and he scraped them off as best he could. Eric and I moved to each side of him and helped lift him to his feet. We slowly let his legs carry his weight.

Team Nike quickly caught up and passed us as Jason walked ahead, carefully testing his injured knee. The rednecks laughed as they passed us which infuriated every member of our team. Eric took a step towards them as he saw the smirks on their faces but then stopped himself as he remembered the rules of the race.

"I'm all right. Let's just take it slow" Jason instructed. We continued on, jogging now, and the crowd went crazy because there was a huge movie screen set up behind the stage where thousands of people were standing. We finished the run well behind Team Nike but we were all very thankful that we had dodged a bullet. As we completed the first leg of the race, we watched ourselves on the big screen. When we began the final quarter mile, Jason started to pick up his pace. I glanced over at him and it was apparent that he wasn't hurt, he was angry. He wasn't really angry at the kids that tripped him as much as he was mad at the rednecks.

As we approached the stage, two paramedics were waiting to attend to Jason. Security was heavy around the stage to prevent any further problems. To the right of the stage, an RV was waiting for us with a police car parked in front of it. Ron Craig was waiting for our arrival at the finish line.

"Are you okay?" Craig asked Jason.

"Yes, I am fine. What's next?" Jason responded.

"Your instructions are waiting for you inside of the RV. You really need to get checked out" Ron said.

"I said that I am fine. Nothing is wrong with me!"

I knew Jason very well and knew that he was a little stubborn when he was angry so I intervened. "He seems to be walking and running fine. Just give us some soap, a wash cloth, some medicine to clean it with, some tweezers and a few bandages. We will make sure that we clean the wound so that it doesn't get infected."

The paramedics responded with amazing speed to my requests. Within two minutes we were boarding the vehicle and waving goodbye to our families and friends.

THE ULTIMATE CHALLENGE

The RV was a Ford E350 Tracker. The sides of the vehicle had been wrapped with The Ultimate Challenge logo. Our new home was very roomy and comfortable. It included an eating table behind the front passenger seat with a long bench seat across from the table. Behind the table was a small kitchen that had a microwave, a sink and eight small cabinets that were fully stocked with food and drinks.

A small hallway contained a bathroom and led to a bedroom in the back of the vehicle. It contained a double bed that could be converted into a couch. Above the bed was a television and DVR player which we were told to play to receive instructions on our next adventure. Jason took a seat on the long bench, sitting on one end and stretching his legs out to begin working on them.

Drew, Eric and I crowded into the small back bedroom to watch the tape. We turned on the television, pressed play on the DVR and appearing before us was John Simmons himself.

"Well boys, did you like that run? Did the fireworks at the beginning of the race scare you? They were supposed to. Your next stop is the Appalachian Trail. It is one of my favorite places in this world. You guys are going hiking this afternoon. A guide will be waiting for you when you get there. You have an atlas provided so that you can find the trail yourself. Have fun out there. It will be a little different than Stone Mountain. You will be lucky if you see anyone out there." He disappeared and we immediately hurried to find the atlas.

I jumped behind the wheel and we received a police escort out of the park and onto highway 78 heading towards Atlanta. We were already behind so we decided to map our route while we were driving. There was a note attached to the atlas that told us we had a governor attached to the vehicle that would not allow us to go over seventy miles per hour. There were small cameras hidden all over the vehicle to capture every move that we made from every angle. The bathroom was our only secret sanctuary.

As we headed up the highway, the policeman veered to the right and we were on our way, leaving the large rock of Stone Mountain and thousands of people in our rear view mirror.

As Drew studied the map, Eric assisted Jason with cleaning his wounds. Eric was accustomed to this, having helped many athletes in their time of need. Eric began removing the pebbles that were still lodged in Jason's knee with tweezers as Jason clinched both sides of the bench that he was sitting on.

"This sucks!" Jason exclaimed. That was about as much emotion as you were ever going to get out of Jason. It had to be painful.

"Quit your crying" Eric answered. "It could have been much worse. You could have torn an ACL and the race would be over already."

Jason was still pretty angry "Did you see those idiots laughing?"

"Oh yeah, I saw them" Eric replied. "I started to go after the big one, but then I remembered that if I touch him we automatically lose. He will get his when we beat their ass." He was always a little high strung but seeing the other team laugh at his fallen teammate was a little more than he could handle. "When this thing is over, I am going to challenge every one of them. They are bringing my inner redneck out."

"Just beat them" Jason replied as he tried to calm down his friend. "We will be the ones laughing in the end. Let them laugh now. We will be laughing all the way to the bank."

Eric continued his work, methodically looking over Jason's knee and I weaved in and out of traffic, eager to reach our next destination.

We thought that hiking might be a big part of the race and we were about to see if all of our training was going to pay off. We mapped out the path that

THE ULTIMATE CHALLENGE

we would be taking on our atlas and the drive was only going to take about an hour and a half because the Appalachian Trail begins in the north Georgia Mountains. The Appalachian Trail was extremely difficult in Georgia. We would face one steep incline after another and our progress would be very slow. It was something that I had always wanted to try. My brother was an avid outdoorsman and had hiked several sections of the trail. I was just amazed at how long it was. It was like two thousand miles long, going through several states, starting in the south part of the country and ending up in the northeast. I wasn't as adventurous as my brother but still fascinated. I had actually read three different books about The Appalachian Trail with each being written by people that had hiked it from beginning to end. Literally thousands of hikers began the hike every year with the intentions of completing the entire thing. The dropout rate was about ninety percent with only a couple of hundred reaching their destination. Many did not even make it out of Georgia. If The Appalachian Trail was the first real test of the race, I couldn't imagine what was coming next. We knew from the beginning that a race for millions of dollars would be no picnic.

After we had our route mapped out, we had a little time to relax and just drive. A ten minute silence was broken when Jason screamed "That hurts!"

"Just shut up and take it like a man!" Eric shouted back.

"If you would just wait a minute before you stick it back in there it wouldn't hurt so bad" Jason responded.

"I can't see what you two are doing back there nor do I want to but I really hope that you are talking about his knee" Drew said while he laughed.

I looked at Drew "You do realize that millions of people just heard you say that, right?"

"Oh yeah, you are so hilarious Drew" Jason sarcastically replied. "I just can't stop laughing at how funny you are."

Drew didn't even miss a beat "Hey man, I hear what I hear, I don't know what you two fairies have going back there and I really don't care. And those weren't my words. I am just repeating what I already heard."

Friendly childish banter was a good sign that we were fresh and in good spirits. But it was only the beginning of the race.

Chapter 11

The drive to the Appalachian Trail seemed like it took forever. We received several waves from cars passing by. It was hard not to be seen with the RV covered in The Ultimate Challenge graffiti. One enthusiastic woman even felt obliged to flash us, which almost caused me to wreck and kill us all. We were all just a little nervous, especially me. I wasn't sure that everyone on my team knew just how tough the Appalachian Trail could be. We had trained hard but hiking the AT was above any training that we had been through. It was also a little bit exhilarating. I think that every person, especially every male, has a fascination of finding out how tough they really are. I knew that I had always wondered that myself. Do you grind through whatever obstacle is in your way or do you cower like a wimp. I always wondered if I ever faced a live or die situation, how I would react. Did I have what it took to dig deep into the depths of my body to make the impossible happen? I figured that we were about to find out.

We arrived at our destination at noon, so we had about six good hours of daylight left. As we pulled into the small parking lot, the first thing that we saw was the redneck's RV. They had beaten us here and were nowhere to be found. My hopes of them getting lost were gone so we were still playing catch up. We parked, quickly exited the camper and jogged over to the group of people that were no doubt in charge of the place.

A beautiful blond in her mid- thirties named Michelle greeted us and immediately started giving us instructions. "Gentlemen, behind me you will find any and every piece of camping equipment ever made. You may choose whatever you wish but please remember that you will be hiking for several days over very rough terrain."

We began to pour over the equipment as quickly as possible. First, we each selected a backpack and then decided what essentials we would need. We grabbed food, water, two small tents, sleeping bags, flashlights, matches and medical supplies. We each grabbed thermal underwear and toboggans, knowing that the temperatures could get very cold in the higher elevations. I decided to grab a roll of toilet paper which wasn't essential but much better than leaves. I also grabbed a toothbrush and toothpaste. I took two extra pair of socks and slipped into a pair of Reebok hiking boots. Before we departed I double checked the medical supplies, making sure that we had a snake bite kit and a shot of adrenaline, the same thing that we now carried with Thomas. Finally, I selected a handgun. Drew saw me put it in my bag.

Drew angrily asked "What is that for?"

"Believe me, we need it."

"My response did not satisfy him. "No, we don't need it. If you don't shoot yourself, you will shoot one of us!"

"I promise that I will keep the safety lock on at all times. You won't even see it, but I am bringing it."

Drew stormed off, knowing that I wouldn't change my mind. And in some ways he was right. My brother Keith told me that you really needed a gun on the trail just in case something happened. He explained that we could run into poisonous snakes or an angry bear, a pack of coyotes and maybe even an eastern cougar. But more important than that, there were escaped convicts that were rumored to be hiding in the Appalachian Mountains. It was the perfect hiding place for someone that did not want to be found. Keith went on to tell me that

THE ULTIMATE CHALLENGE

eighty percent of the hikers on the trail carried some type of firearm. It was the wilderness and we would be in a desolate area with no police and just a few Park Rangers that were trying to cover thousands of square miles of wilderness. Every year, people disappear on the Appalachian Trail and I was not planning on becoming a statistic.

We hit the rugged trail at twelve thirty, leaving civilization behind us. Eric once again led the way and set a brisk pace. Within minutes, our RV had disappeared from sight and we were engulfed by a huge mountain range. It was hill after beautiful hill of greenery and not another human being in sight. We knew that we needed to close the gap between ourselves and the rednecks. I brought up the rear of our group with only the cameraman behind me. I really felt sorry for the cameraman because his camera looked heavy but the Expedition Channel had a team of cameramen prepared to work this leg of the race. They staggered the cameramen every five miles so that they could continually maintain our pace.

We quickly learned that our seventy mile hike was going to be a marathon. Every mountain was huge and the number of hills to climb was countless. The one thing that we did not account for during our training was the weight of our backpacks. It was an amateur mistake but none of us were accomplished overnight hikers. We had all done day hikes to see a waterfall with our families but we did not account for the strain that backpacks would put on us for this race. I quickly felt soreness in my shoulders and lower back. The extra weight definitely slowed us down. Our spirits were high, but as we reached the summit of each hill it was easy to be a little intimidated by the length of our journey. The trail was well marked and easy to follow but I was already exhausted after an hour and a half of brisk hiking.

We hiked in silence for the first two hours of our trip. I spent my time daydreaming about the huge crowds that had watched us that very morning and what an awesome feeling it was a have thousands of people cheering us on. We went from that atmosphere to the most desolate place east of the Mississippi River in a matter of hours. I think that John planned it that way. There was no one to cheer us on now. We had a seventy mile gut check with the lure of millions of dollars and a team that we wanted to beat very badly keeping us going. After spending twenty minutes thinking about Susan and Thomas and how much I already missed them, I decided to break the silence. Drew was directly in front of me and I wanted to patch things up with him.

"How are you holding up?" I asked.

"I am feeling good. How about you?"

"My shoulders are sore, but I am doing fine."

"Sorry about flying off of the handle back there. I just hate guns. I am afraid of them."

"I'm sorry too. The only reason that I insisted on bringing the gun was because my brother told me that it can be really dangerous out here."

"He should know" Drew replied.

"I am no gun expert. I got certified in Tennessee but I never use them. I just pray that we don't need it."

Eric had been silent for as long as he could stand it. "I am glad that you ladies made up. How far are we going to go today?"

"As far as we can" Jason responded. When it looks like it is starting to get dark, we will find a place to camp."

We marched on until just before dark. We received a new cameraman forty five minutes before we stopped so we knew that we had hiked over five miles. That wasn't bad for a short afternoon in this tough terrain. We found a clearing on the top of a mountain and decided to set up camp. We made Jason sit down because we knew that his knee was sore. Eric and Drew pitched the tents so that left me to build the fire. I wanted to build the fire because it has always fascinated me. I love anything that has to do with burning stuff. I scrambled around as quickly as my tired body would allow to gather wood. Easy to burn dead wood was abundant but daylight was not.

Over the course of fifteen minutes, I gathered enough wood to keep a fire burning all night. Later on I was glad that I did gather so much wood because when the sun goes down so does the temperature. Jason had grabbed a small hand saw, so I had him at work cutting wood while I cleared an area for the fire. I used some dry leaves to start the fire and within minutes we were in business. I had the Royal Ambassador's to thank for this. The RA's are kind of like the boy scouts except that they are church based. I attended RA's every Wednesday night as a kid. Back then I could have cared less about learning how to tie a knot but when it was time to learn about how to build a fire, I was all ears.

Everyone was impressed with my fire. I used only one match and it was producing heat within minutes. It was cold but the trees protected us from the wind. Our tents were set up fairly near the fire and we invited the cameraman to join us for dinner. The cameraman had been busy setting up four cameras on tripods that would record our every move throughout the night. Dinner consisted of Ramen noodles and vegetable stew. Not bad for roughing it. The one luxury that we had was the additional water that we could pick up every five miles when the cameramen switched, so we drank all that we could. Extra food was not available, but we had brought too much. The good side of our mistake was that we could eat well and our loads would become lighter as the trip wore on.

After dinner we added a layer of clothes and huddled close to the fire.

"OK Holland, what's the deal with the gun?" Eric asked.

"My brother just told me that we should have one in case we needed it. These mountains can be dangerous."

"I shouldn't have jumped on you like that" Drew added. "I have just got a lot on my mind."

"You did just find out that you are going to be a dad. And we are all under a lot of pressure to win this race" Jason said in an effort to make Drew feel better.

"It's not just that" Drew quietly responded. "I haven't told anyone this. Not even Barbara. But I guess if she is watching, she will know now. You guys know how I like to gamble."

Everyone nodded in agreement as Drew continued "Well, I have become involved in an offshore sports book and I am into them for a lot of money. I started off wiring them money but then they offered me a line of credit which has become the worst mistake of my life."

"Man, you should have called. I would have loaned you some money to pay them off" I said.

Drew continued "You don't understand. I am down big."

"How much?" Eric asked.

"One twenty"

"I can loan you that when the race ends" Eric said. "One hundred twenty bucks is nothing to worry about."

"I wish" Drew said while staring at the fire. "One hundred twenty thousand is what I owe" Drew answered while our eyes all grew to the size of baseballs.

"Now they started putting a lot of pressure on me and I bought thirty days to finish this race, but if we don't win I am finished."

THE ULTIMATE CHALLENGE

"What does finished mean?" Jason asked.

"I'm not sure" Drew replied. "But I am worried. These are people that you don't want to mess with. I really don't know how it happened. I started to lose on NFL games and kept doubling my bet trying to break even and before I knew it, I was down big. They never cut me off and now they have me by the throat. I could sell everything that I have and it wouldn't be one hundred twenty thousand."

"We will win" I said.

"We better" Drew said with a blank stare.

After a few awkward seconds of silence Jason said "How far behind do you think we are?"

"Not far" I answered. "My guess is a couple of miles at the most."

"Regardless of how far behind we are, we need to be humping it by daybreak. We can't waste any time" Eric said.

With that we all decided to turn in. We had just been through an emotional rollercoaster. I was exhausted and the warmth of my sleeping bag was calling me. The temperature outside was forty degrees and getting colder. I was in a tent with Jason, Eric and Drew had a tent and the cameraman had a tent to himself. Our tent was tiny. I had to crawl in on all fours so that I didn't knock it down. I used my jacket for a pillow and rolled out my thermally insulated sleeping bag. I climbed in and immediately felt two rocks protruding from the ground. I laid the gun on my right side and Jason was on my left. I turned the cell phone from ringer to vibrate because I hate loud noises waking me up in the middle of the night. I attached the phone to my pants then laid back to recall the day's events before nodding off to sleep after fifteen minutes.

Chapter 12

We awoke the next morning to Jason's alarm on his watch playing Mozart. It was still dark outside and it took a few minutes for me to realize where I was. I sat up in the tent and my head scraped the roof. Drew was up quickly and wanting to talk to all of us.

"Let's go. Up and at em" he said.

There is nothing that I hate worse than a morning person. I ignored Drew but did manage to crawl out of the tent and found a nice tree so that I could take a leak. It was freezing outside and our fire had already burned out so we were eager to get moving to warm our bodies. Breakfast consisted of apples and bananas. I ate while Jason packed and within minutes we were off on day two of The Ultimate Challenge.

We walked for the first thirty minutes with a flashlight leading the way before the sun finally broke through the trees to give us some light. We were all sore from the extremely steep inclines but the longer that we walked, the more that our muscles loosened up. We hiked continuously for four hours, trying to close the gap between ourselves and the rednecks. We were making our way up one of the countless hills when the vibrator went off on the cell phone. I unhooked it from my belt and answered without breaking stride.

"Hello" I began.

"Mark, this is Ron Craig."

"Hi Ron."

"Mark, the other team is in trouble. One of them was stung by a bee and he is having a dangerous allergic reaction. Did you guys bring an epi-pen?"

"Yes we did Ron. Where are they?"

"They are about two miles ahead of you but they are headed your way. We have a doctor in route by helicopter but without that shot, he could die."

"I'm on my way."

I dropped the pack from my shoulders and tore into the main compartment. I was throwing the contents of my backpack in every direction. My team members heard the alarm in my voice and were now circled around me, waiting for my response.

"What's wrong?" Jason asked.

"One of the rednecks was stung by a bee and he is having a bad reaction. If I don't get this shot to him, he could die."

I found the shot while I was speaking and took off in a full sprint without another word to my team. My legs were burning after the first one hundred yards of my sprint because it was straight uphill. After about three quarters of a mile, I could see the other team headed my way. Their leader, Ronnie, was carrying Larry over his shoulder and was struggling to jog towards me. I continued sprinting down a steep mountain, almost falling several times with my momentum trying to flip me. When Ronnie saw me, he laid Larry on the ground and began waving both arms in the air. I knew the seriousness of the situation and my thoughts turned to Thomas and the fact that I prayed every night that I

THE ULTIMATE CHALLENGE

would never have to face this situation again. The rednecks were no longer my enemies. I would help anyone that was in trouble.

I finally reached them and struggled to speak between taking gasps of air. Larry was in rough shape. His eyes were swollen shut, his entire face was swollen and he was wheezing heavily. His airway would be completely swollen shut in just a couple of minutes without the shot.

"Pull his pants down!" I commanded.

"What?" Ronnie asked while breathing even heavier than I was.

"Pull his damn pants down now!" Ronnie was a little alarmed at the sound of urgency in my voice.

"Poor Larry laid on the ground, unable to move. Ronnie took care of his pants while I pulled the shot out of the box and shook it up. I had memorized this routine before for Thomas but could function much better now because I wasn't dealing with my precious baby boy.

I put the shot on Larry's leg, flush with his left thigh and pushed, keeping the needle inserted for several seconds. I had the procedure memorized, hoping that I would never have to do it to my son. I then pulled the needle out of his leg and exchanged nervous glances with Ronnie. I then sat down, still trying to catch my breath, and intensely studied Larry's face.

"Larry, I have given you a shot of adrenaline. You have had an acute allergic reaction to the bee sting and this shot will help you breath better. Just hang in there. It will start working any second now."

We sat back and waited. Both Ronnie and I were covered in sweat. We continued watching Larry, praying for a sign of relief. After about thirty seconds he spoke "I think it is working." The shot was a miracle worker. Within minutes, the swelling in his throat and face started to go down and Larry slowly came back to life. Their other two teammates arrived soon after.

"Doctor is about ten minutes out. The helicopter landed and he is driving in on a four wheeler" Doug said with their cell phone in hand.

A few minutes later my team arrived with Eric carrying my pack. "Do you guys need anything else?" I asked.

No one answered. So we were off. No thank you. No nothing.

We were still within their earshot when my temper got the best of me. "I just saved that guy's life, so you're welcome."

We were in the lead now so at least we accomplished something. My angry temper was sending terrible thoughts through my mind. Thoughts that I should have just let him die and we would win the race. Then the good side of my conscious answered with the fact that I could never do that. For the first time in my life, I had actually saved someone's life. There was definitely a feeling of accomplishment that went along with that. Never mind the fact that the guy that I saved was a no good, disrespectful piece of crap that laughed at my friend when he was hurt and my main goal in life was to make sure that he continued living a life of poverty. I wanted to let him live and ruin his dreams all at the same time. We continued hiking but I was exhausted from running. I was just thankful that we were on an emotional high because we were in the lead. We were winning and also hoping that the doctor arriving behind us would meticulously check his patient. We were going to use every second to push forward and widen the gap. We maintained a steady pace, slow enough to allow us to waste a little energy on speaking.

"That guy looked awful" Jason said.

"Yeah" I replied. "You should have seen him before the shot."

THE ULTIMATE CHALLENGE

"You couldn't even recognize him" Drew added.

"Holland, don't you hate needles?" Eric asked.

"Yes, I do hate needles. It was just one of those things that you do out of instinct and adrenaline."

"How long do you think they will be there?" Jason asked.

"Not long. That medicine is amazing. Once you have counteracted the reaction, you are usually fine. They will try to get him to rest and check his vital signs, but knowing those guys, they will just start hiking again."

We stopped for lunch and ate in ten minutes before continuing our journey. It felt so good to sit down. I took my shoes off while we ate and the tingling in my feet felt so good if only for a few minutes. My feet ached, my shoulders were raw from the backpack straps and my legs felt heavy. But the thought of winning twenty five million dollars each was pretty darn good motivation. I'll rest in my new mansion.

Chapter 13

As we arrived at our campsite for the second night, we rested for twenty minutes before doing anything with the impending darkness as our only motivation to work. A full day of hiking on the Appalachian Trail could exhaust even the most experienced hiker. I gathered our wood more slowly than the previous day and was not quite as excited to build a fire.

After setting up camp and getting the fire going we took another rest, putting off dinner for an hour while we untied our hiking boots and enjoyed feeling our feet tingle. Someone was smart enough to bring Ben Gay and my legs and feet were happy to have it. I don't know what it is in Ben Gay that makes your aching muscles feel so good, but the stuff really works. I just wish that Susan was here to rub it in. My thoughts turned to my family as I wondered what Thomas was doing and if he was asking about me.

We warmed up a pot of chilli and we ate it with Saltine crackers. The chilli hit the spot as the temperatures once again dipped into the forties. Anything would have tasted good because after a full day of hiking, we were famished.

Jason and Drew were engulfed in a conversation about abortion so I decided to talk to Eric.

"So how is married life treating you?"

"Honestly, I don't know."

"What do you mean that you don't know? You are still a newlywed. You are supposed to be going at it like bunnies and walking around with a goofy grin on your face all of the time."

"The first two months were like that but it seems like lately all that we do is argue."

"What about?"

"Mostly money. She is really a tight wad with money and you know that I spend everything that I get. And she complains about the long hours that I work during football season. Then when I do get a day off, she spends it with her friends just to prove a point."

"That's tough" I said and before I could say another word he continued talking.

"And her mom likes to poke her nose into it. That lady gets on my nerves. I think that her mom doesn't like me. She wishes that Jessica would have married somebody with money. Of course they are both happy now that we may be filthy rich, I just don't know" he said while bowing his head in defeat.

"Do you love her?"

"I love the girl that I married, but everything is different now."

"The first year can be rough."

"To be honest with you, I am glad that we are having this time apart. It will give both of us some time to think. But I can say right now that I have not missed her for one second. I'm just glad to get away from her nagging."

THE ULTIMATE CHALLENGE

"You may feel differently in a few weeks" I said.

"Maybe" Eric unconvincingly replied.

By this time Jason and Drew's conversation about abortion was starting to wake up every animal within five miles. Drew was pro-life, Jason was pro-choice and they were both determined to argue their position. I was tired of listening to them so I decided to throw my two cents into the mix.

"Guys. Guys. May I address the court?"

They both smiled. "Go ahead" Drew answered.

"It's obvious that you guys are never going to agree on this issue. Our country is split fifty-fifty just like you. It will always be like that. We aren't going to change it here in the middle of no-where at a camp fire. When people are fifty-fifty on something, you have to find a compromise. I think that is what is wrong with our country right now. We have two parties with the loud ten percent on each side radically against each other.

The other eighty percent fall somewhere in the middle and don't like to argue about every single thing. There has to be a compromise somewhere in the middle. Not just about abortion, but about everything. We elect lifetime politicians that get a pension that lasts the rest of their lives and we sit back and allow them to accomplish nothing and reap the rewards. No bill is passed without lots of little attachments to it. That is what is considered compromise. It is just kind of disgusting to me. Go ahead with your argument. My ranting is over."

The conversation thankfully turned more casual for the rest of the evening with a big debate about whether college athletes should be paid and if Major League Baseball had a tough enough stance on performance enhancing drugs. We also argued a little bit on who the best looking female professional athlete was. It was fun for us to argue sometimes, especially about sports because it wasn't as much of a hot button issue as politics. It took our minds off of being exhausted for a while.

Day three of The Ultimate Challenge was very cold. I woke up at 5:30 A.M. because my nose was freezing. I quietly climbed out of the tent and found an apple. We had hiked almost twenty miles the day before and by my calculations there were forty four miles to go. Only forty four miles. I put on some deodorant but it was a futile attempt. I smelled raunchy but at least everyone else did also. I thought about Susan, sound asleep in our comfortable bed with a warm down comforter.

One of the great things about getting married is that women know exactly what you need to make a bed feel awesome. Susan introduced me to a feather bed, down comforter, down pillows, satin sheets and velvet comforter covers. I always complained about how much she spent on bedding but I never complained about how good it felt. I could almost feel it, sinking into comfort as you lay down with two fluffy pillows under your head. The other thing that Susan taught me about bedding is that you should wash your sheets once a week. In college, my sheets only got washed when I went home for the holidays. Eric once went an entire year without washing his sheets.

The other guys started stirring and by 6:15 we were on the trail again, inching closer to the end of our hike. We walked in single file. Eric, Jason, Drew, myself and then the cameraman bringing up the rear. About two hours into our hike we were all startled when Eric stopped in his tracks.

"Whoa" he said.

About thirty yards in front of us and twenty five yards to the right of the trail we saw a black bear. She hadn't seen us yet.

"What do we do?" Jason asked with alarm in his voice.

"Don't run" I answered. "We are supposed to make noise so that we don't surprise it."

"Wait a minute!" Drew quietly exclaimed. "Look in that tree above the bear."

In an oak tree about thirty feet above the bear sat two cute little cubs.

"We have got to be careful. She will be more aggressive with those babies around" I said.

"Let's just take off and run past it" Eric said.

"No way" I answered. "That bear can run a lot faster than you."

Jason then took a leadership role. The bear still hadn't noticed us. "Let's just veer off of the trail, away from the bear and walk like normal."

Everyone nodded in agreement. We walked about twenty yards left of the trail, with all eyes on the bear. The cameraman now focused all of his attention and his camera on the bear. He was not watching where he was going and tripped over a stump, falling on the ground. His camera banged loudly on a tree as he fell which caused the bear to raise her head and stare directly at us. She was about forty yards away from us, definitely within reach if she wanted to make us dinner.

We all stopped in our tracks as the cameraman lifted himself off of the ground and dusted himself off. He picked up the heavy camera and then pointed it directly at the bear. His sudden movement alarmed her and she let out an extremely loud roar and showed us her deadly teeth. Now I was scared.

The bear immediately took a defensive stance by standing on her two back legs. She was almost as tall as we were when she stood. The roar was ferocious as it echoed throughout the forest. We were close enough to see that her claws were razor sharp as her attempt to intimidate us was very successful.

"Stand your ground" I nervously whispered. I had seen a documentary on black bears on the Discovery Channel. "Let's keep talking and walk slowly." As we started to walk, the bear took a step toward us, no doubt in an attempt to protect her cubs. We continued walking slowly, talking nervously, and attempting to avoid a conflict. My gun was somewhere in my pack, but I had no idea where. The bear let out another grunt and took another step toward us. We were all sweating now, wanting to run, but knowing that running would be the absolute worst thing to do.

The cameraman had seen enough. He stopped filming the bear and actually started walking to our left, between us and the angry mom. He could have cared less about his job, he was concerned for his life. We kept walking with the leaves crunching under our feet with every step. The bear continued her awesome stare with her head upright, watching every move. Finally, she decided to spare us and the further we got away from her, the faster we walked. We passed the bear and as she slowly disappeared from our sight and we could breathe again. We took a glance back with every few steps, fearing the worst but thankfully finding nothing. We had dodged another bullet.

We continued hiking briskly for two more hours, skipping our normal ten minute break to get as much distance as possible between ourselves and the angry bear. As the day wore on, the temperature reached a balmy sixty three degrees and I shed a layer of clothes for every two miles that we hiked. We loved having a new cameraman stationed every five miles because it was an easy way for us to determine the distance that we had traveled.

At 4:00 P.M. we reached our third cameraman of the day. That meant that we had traveled fifteen miles with two and a half hours of daylight left. When we got to the cameraman change we decided to take a break and rest our weary legs. I found a tree and leaned against it, resting my pack on a neighboring pine

THE ULTIMATE CHALLENGE

tree. I had developed a painful blister on the ball of my left foot so I took my shoe off to examine the damage. As soon as I removed my shoe, I could see blood all over my sock.

"Holland, that looks painful." Eric said with a grin. For some reason Eric always laughed when other people were in pain. He had been that way since I met him. He wasn't doing it to be mean, that was just his reaction and it was kind of annoying.

I didn't respond, I was too tired to answer. I wiped the blood off as best I could and then applied a large band aid. I then wrapped a cloth around my foot before adding two pair of socks and then my shoes. I had no idea what was best, but this seemed like a good idea. I was not going to let a blister slow us down. I wanted to get my mind off of the problem.

"Twenty nine miles left" I said.

"I just hope that whatever we do next does not involve walking" Jason responded.

"I'm drained" Drew added. "I'm just out of gas."

"Me too" I responded. "My foot is killing me and I haven't slept good yet."

"We are over half way there and in the lead, so you pansies just need to suck it up" Eric explained.

We no longer noticed the beautiful scenery around us. We no longer cared about millions of people watching us. All that I was concentrating on was my next step. I looked down as we hiked, counting my paces one hundred steps at a time. I counted one hundred paces then stuck one finger out. Then I counted one hundred more and stuck a second finger out. I did it for all ten fingers then started over. The pain in my foot persisted, so it was time to play another mind game. I thought of different cities and who their professional sports teams were. Dallas – Cowboys, Rangers, Mavericks, Stars. Chicago – Cubs, Whitesox, Bulls, Bears and Blackhawks. This game worked. It took me to another world, a world with a couch, a remote and ESPN.

We made camp at 6:15 with darkness approaching quickly. I set up the tent while Jason built the fire. We had covered eighteen miles on the day so we only had twenty six to go. We were almost seeing light at the end of this winding, twisting tunnel. We were starting to become more proficient at setting up our camp. We finished well before Earl, our new cameraman. After setting things up we laid back, rested our feet and watched Earl earn his money by finding the most interesting angles to catch our events that night.

Dinner sucked. It was dehydrated beef stew. You just add water, heat it up and then enjoy an awful tasting meal. But we were starved and ate every bit. After dinner every night we looked forward to finding out what the topic for us to argue about would be. No matter how tired we were, we all loved to argue with each other. Tonight's topic was baseball.

Eric said "What were the Yankees thinking by giving A-Rod a ten year contract like that?"

"I honestly have no idea" I answered. He had already been caught once using steroids so who knows how good he really is now. The Yankees have the biggest television market by far and he used to put butts in seats but now they are regretting it big time."

"Yeah but twenty plus million a year is ridiculous" Jason replied.

Drew then jumped in "Now wait a minute. Tom Cruise can make twenty five million dollars for every movie he makes and nobody says a word. The best boxers predetermine their payday before the fight ever happens. A player should be worth how much money they bring in."

THE ULTIMATE CHALLENGE

"You have got to hand it to Major League Baseball" I said. Their revenue sharing program is actually starting to work. Teams like the Pirates can compete now. You don't have to live in a huge media market to be good. It's good for baseball. They just need to stiffen penalties for performance enhancing drugs quite a bit and they are sitting pretty."

"You're still going to have big market teams like the Dodgers and Yankees outspending everybody" Jason replied.

"The Angels have gone crazy too" I said. "But at the end of the day and with a second wild card spot open, the game is pretty good."

Eric was bored to death because he could care less about baseball and he went on to bed. A large clap of thunder soon chased us all to our tents and a heavy rain began to fall. The pitch blackness of night had made each of us unaware of the approaching storm. We each made our way to our tents, being careful not to touch the sides as we climbed in so that the rain would not seep through. The storm was strong and made a grand entrance as it approached our camp. Thunder rumbled throughout the forest and bolts of lightning lit the darkened sky. Our tent was our safe haven, or so we thought.

The lightning flash increased and the thunder grew louder as the center of the storm approached. God was angry with someone and he was taking it out on the land around us. Jason and I were silent, hoping that our metal tent poles would not attract a dangerous bolt of electricity. The rain was heavy and loud but the trees around us provided a shield for the brunt of the water. Our rain tarp was also doing its job.

All of a sudden our pitch black campsite was lit up like it was the middle of day. We then heard a crash of thunder and an explosion. The noise was deafening. Seconds later we began to hear the cracking sound of breaking wood. It started fairly quietly at first and then grew louder and louder as the tree that had been struck by the bolt of lightning started gaining momentum as it fell. I closed my eyes and clinched my fists, knowing that death was certain if the tree landed on our tent. Limbs were cracking and breaking. Leaves were whistling as the tree was falling to the ground. The tree finally landed with a huge bang and the ground around us literally shook as it landed.

"Are you guys okay?" I yelled to the other tent.

"What about you Earl?" Jason asked our cameraman.

"I am fine" he answered.

Jason sat up and stuck his head outside of the tent and saw a huge oak that had fallen and was splintered at the base. It landed about twenty feet from our tent. Once again we were lucky. Mother Nature had decided to spare us.

As quickly as the thunderstorm had come, it was gone. We could all breathe easier, as I laid back down. Jason was on my left, the gun on my right and the cell phone was attached to my pants with the ringer on vibration. It was silent in our camp and I felt like I could finally get some sleep.

I entered my first deep sleep since the race began. A sleep so deep that you don't remember dreaming, turning over or anything else about your surroundings. And it felt great. My body yearned for this type of rest to recover from the rigorous beating that it had taken over the past few days. For the first time on the Appalachian Trail, I felt safe. The bears were behind us, the storm had passed and nothing else could go wrong. If I only knew.

Chapter 14

I woke up disoriented, completely unaware of my surroundings until I sat up and my head scraped the top of our tiny two man tent. It was pitch dark inside and out. Jason was sound asleep, quietly snoring with his back to me. My phone was ringing with the vibrations tickling my side. I had no idea how long it had been ringing because I am extremely difficult to wake up from a deep sleep. My thoughts quickly turned to Thomas and Susan and I prayed that they were okay. I quickly unfastened the phone from my pants and pressed the answer button.

I answered quietly so that I wouldn't wake up Jason.

"Hello" I whispered.

"Mark, don't say another word. This is Ron Craig. Is your gun near you? Answer me softly."

My heart sank as my blood pressure shot up. "Yes" I answered as quietly as I could.

"Get it now and take the safety off."

I was momentarily paralyzed in fear by Ron's order to stay silent. A numbing adrenaline rush overcame my body as I feared what would come out of his mouth next. I immediately shook off my sleepiness and was wide awake. My heart was beating so hard that it seemed as though I could hear it.

Ron continued "Mark, you need to stay calm. The cameras have picked up an intruder in your camp. We have confirmed that it is not a member of the other team. He is carrying a large knife and we think that he has a gun strapped to the left side of his pants. Oh My God! He is going into the cameraman's tent!"

Earl's tent was about thirty feet directly in front of ours. I slowly and silently unzipped our tent, poked my head out and looked straight ahead. Luckily, the skies had cleared and the illumination from the half-moon allowed me to see fairly clearly. I focused my eyes on Earl's tent while listening for anything, hearing nothing. I then let my guard down a bit, thinking that this is just a scheme dreamed up by John Simmons as part of the race. This was just John at his best, playing practical jokes. It was then that my fantasy became reality as I saw Earl's tent move. My relief was gone and the fear returned.

I jumped in surprise as Ron spoke again. "I am watching your campsite on a live feed. Mark, you need to distract that guy and get him out of that tent now!"

I could tell by the alarm in Ron Craig's voice that this was no joke. I finished unzipping the tent and began crawling out. When my head had cleared the top of the tent, I lunged forward to stand while keeping the gun pointed in the direction of the intruder. My eyes were now completely adjusted to the dark and I could see very well, although everything seemed more black and white than in color. I took one step toward Earl's tent then did a quick three hundred and sixty degree turn to make sure that the intruder did not have any accomplices. I saw nothing unusual, but Earl's tent was too quiet. I decided to do as Ron had asked. Before I said a word, I picked up the cell phone off of the ground where I had placed it and whispered "What if he comes after me?"

"Then shoot him! You have to protect yourself."

THE ULTIMATE CHALLENGE

With no other hesitation I screamed "Hey, what are you doing? Get out of the tent, now!"

Just as I had feared, Earl's tent came to life. No words were spoken but the tent was moving in every direction. I took two steps forward as my finger massaged the trigger of the gun. My hands were shaking as I was praying that Earl would exit the tent. The front flap opened and a figure began to appear. I could hear my friends stirring in the background and I was silently begging for them to help me.

As the intruder exited the tent, I could see that it wasn't Earl. The man had long hair and a large unkempt beard.

"What are you doing?" I screamed as loud as I could.

I received no response as the stranger exited the tent and stood straight up, directly facing me about twenty feet away. The knife was in his right hand and I could see a dark substance dripping from the end.

"Stay right there and don't move. Earl, can you hear me?"

The intruder still didn't speak, he just stood without uttering a sound.

My teammates were all awake but still dazed and confused. I could hear Jason getting out of the tent. His movement startled the intruder and he made a quick move of his left hand to his side. It was then that I remembered that he might have a gun. I aimed my revolver at his left shoulder and squeezed the trigger. The gun let out a tremendous boom and instantaneously the intruder was hit. My shot had missed the intended target but had hit the intruder in his left side. He leaned down and covered the wound with his right hand. Before I could say a word, he raised up and started running towards me. The first bullet had only missed his heart by inches but he seemed unfazed. I reacted by shooting again and the second bullet pierced his upper right leg and he immediately fell to his knees. He dropped his knife as both hands hit the ground, bracing him on his knees.

Our campsite was utter chaos as Jason, Drew and Eric were all screaming with no idea of what was going on. The reverberations of the second gunshot were still echoing throughout the mountains and in my ears so I couldn't hear anything for a few seconds. I approached the intruder who was still balanced on his hands and knees. He was moaning ever so slightly, trying to keep his pain to himself. I didn't want him on all fours because I couldn't monitor his every move. I took two steps forward and with all of the might that my left leg could muster, I kicked the man squarely in the forehead. The kick made a disgusting thumping sound like when you bounce a deflated basketball on the ground and it doesn't bounce. The intruder's head whipped back and his body followed as he landed on the ground with his face to the sky.

"If you move one inch, the next one is going between your eyes" I said with the barrel of my gun staring him boldly in the face."

"Somebody get a flashlight and check on Earl. He has been stabbed. Someone else find a rope and some bandages."

Jason ran to our tent to get the flashlight and Drew went to get bandages. Eric stood behind me, both of us speechless, staring at our wounded enemy.

I interrupted the silence "He's got a gun tucked in his pants on the left side. I'll keep the gun on him and you check him over."

Eric cautiously began the process of patting down the stranger, finding his gun and another knife. I kept the gun pointed directly at his eyes, ready to fire if he made a move.

Jason quickly returned with the flashlight. "Jason go check on Earl."

THE ULTIMATE CHALLENGE

"I went to get the flashlight. You check on him."

"I'm holding the gun" I sternly replied.

Jason responded with "I can't hold the gun, I don't know how to use it." Jason was petrified, as we all were. No one wanted any part of this.

Finally, Eric took control "Here give me the gun Mark and you go check on Earl."

I gave my meanest glance to Jason and jerked the flashlight out of his hands. I reluctantly handed Eric the gun and slowly made my way to Earl's tent. I didn't want to check on Earl, nobody did. No sound was coming from his tent and there was a lot of blood on the intruder's knife.

I opened the flap to Earl's tent very methodically, performing every step possible to avoid shining my flashlight in his face. I bent down, tried to gather my composure, held my breath and after letting my flashlight lead the way, stuck my head inside the tent. The circle that my flashlight created was focused directly on the cameraman's face. The sight that I saw would haunt me for years to come. The intruder had clearly slashed Earl's throat from jawbone to jawbone. His eyes were open and staring at me and a beard of blood had formed under his neck. The blood beard extended onto his clothes and into his sleeping bag. He was dead, there was no question about it.

I survived the initial shock of the gruesome sight, but my second glance didn't fare so well. I sprung out of my crotched position just inside of the tent. As my head exited, so did my dinner from the previous night. By the second heave, I managed to get on all fours just outside of the tent.

Drew finally returned with the bandages. Eric had his eyes fixed on the murderer and Jason nervously paced around the campsite. No one even asked me about Earl's status, they didn't have to. My actions spoke for themselves.

"Jason, please go get the cell phone that is laying by our tent on the ground" I muttered with the lingering taste of vomit engulfing my throat.

The vomiting had stopped but the nausea hadn't. But it was time for me to step up to the plate and be a leader. My teammates were all staring at me for instructions. Jason handed me the phone and Ron Craig was on the line.

"Earl is dead" I stated.

"I figured as much" Mr. Craig replied. "I have been watching everything in real time. We have park rangers, the local sheriff and EMS on the way. They are coming in on four wheelers but they are still about an hour away. There is nowhere to land a helicopter. Leave Earl's tent alone because it is a crime scene now and do what you can to stop the guy's bleeding. Please be careful with him and don't let your guard down. We will get through this Mark. Just try to stay calm."

"Stay calm? Stay calm? What do you mean stay calm? One guy is dead and his killer is dying. We were almost killed out here and you say stay calm?"

"I am really sorry Mark. Really sorry. We never dreamed that anything like this would ever happen."

I hung up the phone and looked at my friends. They were in total disbelief just as I was. "Drew, we need to wrap the bandages around his wounds so he doesn't bleed to death. Will you do it?"

"Yeah, as long as Eric keeps that gun pointed at his head" Drew replied.

Jason looked at me with anger in his eyes. "Why did you have to shoot him?"

A fury entered my body like none that I had ever felt.

"What did you just say?" I said stressing every word.

THE ULTIMATE CHALLENGE

I paused for a few seconds before continuing. "Why don't you enter that tent right there and you will see why I shot the son of a bitch!"

Jason answered quickly "You still didn't have to shoot him. Why didn't you just show him your gun?"

I was holding back with all of my might. Every bone in my body wanted to punch Jason right in the face. I could explain to him that the guy had gone for his gun, but I needed to cool off. I paused for a few seconds then approached my good friend still full of anger, fear and disbelief.

Our noses were about two inches apart. I spoke to him in complete and total anger. "I am going to tell you this one time. I don't have to explain anything to you. You better turn your butt around and walk away from here. And if you don't, I will put you in the morgue too."

Eric saw the argument unfolding and came over to break us up and Drew continued to tend to the murderer's wounds. Eric stepped in between us and said "Guys we are in a terrible situation. Mark, you did what you had to do. You both need to ….."

Jason's eyes were as big as softballs as his focus turned to Drew. The murderer had taken advantage of our argument and now had a death grip on Drew's throat. Our friend couldn't breathe or manage to tear the murderer's hands off of his throat. Jason rushed to the scene with Eric and myself right behind him. The murderer was sitting up, leaned over Drew and applying pressure with all of his might to the grip that he had on Drew's throat. Drew was on his back with both hands clutched on the murderer's forearm, trying desperately to release the death grip. Drew's face was motionless, his eyes were open wide. Jason noticed that the murderer's mid-section was exposed and with a ten foot head start he kicked the guy in the groin with a mighty blow that any placekicker would be proud of. The murderer immediately lost his grip on Drew's neck and rolled over in pain with both hands on his crotch. Eric then joined in on the assault by swiftly kicking the guy in his back. I ran to Drew, still motionless and clutching his throat.

"Calm down buddy" I said while bending down and putting my arm around his back. "Just take slow deep breaths, in and out, in and out."

Eric's anger increased as he kicked the murderer again causing the man to fall on his back. "I should just waste him right now!" Eric shouted.

"No Eric, we are in control now" Jason pleaded.

"Jason, go get the rope. It's in my pack" I said.

Drew slowly caught his breath and within a few minutes, he was in a sitting position with his elbows on his knees and his hands covered his face. I knew Drew well and it was best to leave him alone at a time like this. He would let us know if he needed anything.

I turned my attention to the murderer. He was moaning in pain but still had not uttered a word. He knew now that he was defeated. He had two gunshot wounds, a welp on his forehead and his testicles had swollen to the size of grapefruits. Regardless, we were not taking any chances. Jason returned with the rope and with Eric pointing the gun at our prisoner, we tied both of his hands and feet together. It was still dark outside and we had no idea of the time.

We formed a circle around our prisoner, waiting for help to arrive. Drew was normally a very peaceful person but he was enraged like I had never seen before. He stared at the prisoner, daring the wounded animal to make a move. I carefully applied bandages as everyone else watched, ready to come to my rescue if needed. Drew taunted the guy by taking a burning log from the fire. "How would this feel against you skin, huh?" Drew said as he waved the flames just inches from the stranger's face. But the murderer didn't flinch or even make a sound.

THE ULTIMATE CHALLENGE

"Drew as much as I would love to see it, you can't torture him, this is all on television" I said. Drew ignored my warning. He had turned into a madman. I had never seen Drew raise his hand in anger, not even once. He was one of the nicest people that I had ever met. But he had stared death in the face and now he was confronting his attacker. He had an eerie look in his eyes and we all saw it, even our prisoner.

Jason approached Drew "Why don't you take a little walk to cool off. We will watch him."

Drew also ignored Jason and never took his eyes off of the attacker. I was beginning to worry about what he might do. Eric, holding the gun, was also glancing nervously at our friend.

Eric said "Drew, man, the cops will be here soon and this idiot will get what's coming to him. Let's just drop it."

Drew slowly grinned, with his eyes never leaving his attacker. The grin was evil. We could see that his mind was working but we had no idea what it was telling him to do.

The look in his eyes was creeping me out. "Drew, listen to me, don't do something that you will regret later. You have a baby on the way." He didn't respond to me so I yelled "Listen to me!"

I finally got his attention and his head turned to me. "Drew, it's just not worth it."

Drew turned back to the murderer. "I'm not going to hurt our little friend here" he said in his most pleasant voice. "I'm just going to give him a little bath, he looks dirty."

Drew then proceeded to undo his belt, unbutton his pants and drop them. We all took a step back and the murderers eyes grew as big as golf balls. The murderer was shaking his head no, which caused Drew to bellow out a tremendously wicked laugh that echoed throughout the mountains. He took one step towards the murderer and then proceeded to urinate on the man's face. Next, he moved onto the man's hair and then he finished by moving up and down, up and down, soaking the murderer from head to toe. He finally finished and then let out two more small squirts just for fun. He then pulled up his boxers, pulled up his pants, zipped up his pants, buckled his belt and said "There, that's better." He then walked a little closer to the murderer that was gagging while having his hands and legs tied. "You try to kill me, so I piss on your face. You better hope that I don't have to take a dump because I will not hesitate to do that either. Fair is fair." Drew then turned around and walked away.

Chapter 15

Eric, Jason and I were stunned as was our prisoner. The man was shaking his head from side to side like a dog trying to dry off after a bath. My friends and I stared at him with our heads down. Then I made the mistake of glancing at Eric. Then I made another mistake of glancing at Jason. We all then stared directly down at the ground, trying with all of our might not to start laughing. There was nothing funny about this. A guy was dead. Another was seriously injured. But Eric couldn't hold it any longer. We all ended up busting out laughing, not for long, but we all did laugh. It was just like when someone farted in church. It wasn't politically correct at all. The world would think that we were terrible people. Our wives would think that we had gone mad. No one would understand it, but it was either laugh or cry and in every terrible situation that I have ever been in with these great friends of mine, we have chosen to laugh.

Help arrived thirty minutes later. Two paramedics, six park rangers and four policemen drive in on four wheelers. We were elated to first hear their engines then see their headlights. We did not want the responsibility of guarding the murderer. They arrived on the scene with Sheriff Rob Manning in charge.

"Are you boys all right?" he asked.

"Yes sir" we responded.

"We will take over from here. I have to take you boys into the station for some questioning, but since we have it all on video tape, we should we able to wrap it up in a few hours and let you get back to your race. Where is Mr. Holland?"

I raised my hand as the Sheriff continued "Mr. Holland, I will need you to give me your gun as evidence. It was clearly a case of self-defense but I need it anyway."

Eric gave the Sheriff our gun and we climbed on the back of the four wheelers, which were driven by Park Rangers. The first signs of daylight were beginning to approach as we made the one hour trip to the Sheriff's station. The Sheriff was going to be about one hour behind us. He had to organize the crime scene and instruct his deputies on what to do. The extra hour that we would have proved to be invaluable to us.

We arrived at the Sheriff's station after a very cold and bumpy ride through the mountains. The office was heated and a pot of coffee was waiting for us. Despite the circumstances, it was nice to be inside a warm building again. We thawed out our bodies, rested our weary legs and filled our hungry stomachs with warm coffee and sausage biscuits.

We rested in the break room. It was generic in appearance, just like the rest of the Sheriff's office. It was built in the late 1970's and had not been renovated since. We sat in silence, staring at the crème colored walls with no pictures or windows. We had one vending machine and a coffee pot to look at. We sat around a brown rectangular table with silver metal legs.

Drew had not spoken since peeing on our prisoner and we didn't dare speak to him, fearing that his evil twin would answer. He actually broke the silence. "It's daylight. We are going to be playing catch up after we finally get out of here. I hope that stupid Sheriff shows up."

THE ULTIMATE CHALLENGE

"What happened to you up there?" Eric daringly asked him.

"What do you mean what happened? I had to take a leak."

And that was that. No one asked him about his brief period of insanity again. We all accepted his explanation and no one dared to press him on it. A deputy approached and asked us if we would like to take a shower and all four of us jumped at once.

The shower was exactly the right answer for my misery. I was filthy and the hot water spraying my body gave me a renewed energy. I had already forgotten what it was like to be clean and it was a feeling that I would never take for granted again. Feeling clean felt like I was born again. It was so refreshing. A bar of soap was my new best friend.

With showers complete, we all felt much better. We were all in pretty good spirits because we were alive, in one piece and getting cleaned up gave each of us a renewed vigor. All of us except for Jason I should say. Jason had reverted into his own world. He did not speak unless spoken to and he gave us one word answers to our questions. He was really shaken up and understandably so.

After waiting for what seemed like a full day, we were all getting restless in the break room so we all decided to take a stroll around the office. When we reached the front room, we noticed four news trucks. There was one from every major network. We went back into the break room to avoid the press and after five nervous minutes of waiting, Ron Craig entered the room.

"Hello gentlemen" he said as we all nodded our reply.

"I decided to come up here in person to make sure that you all are alright. The Sheriff is right behind me and we both wanted to meet with you."

In walked Sheriff Manning, an overweight man in his fifties. He was bald on the top of his head with very close cut gray hair around the sides. They both took their seats adjacent to us in the break room.

The Sheriff began "I am glad to see that you boys got cleaned up. We have already got a fingerprint match on our prisoner. Have you ever heard the name John Albert Henley?"

The name definitely sounded familiar but I wasn't sure where I had heard it. The Sheriff continued "We have been looking for this guy for over five years. He is one of the FBI's most wanted fugitives. He is a known serial killer. He went on a killing spree throughout the Midwest and then he disappeared. We had the best law enforcement officials in the country looking for this guy and nothing turned up. You boys are heroes."

"When can we get back to the race?" Eric asked. We could be heroes later. Right now, we had a race to win.

"You will be out of here in less than an hour. Then it will be an hour back to where we picked you up" the Sheriff explained.

The Sheriff asked several questions about the incident including what we were doing before it happened, why I shot the guy, if we had any criminal history etc. etc. After half an hour, Sheriff Manning had all of the information that he needed. He told us that John Henley was in stable condition and would pull through. He then left the room so that Ron could speak to us.

Chapter 16

"Guys, I know that this has been an extremely traumatic experience for you. If you decide to end the race right now, I would completely understand. But if you do continue, there will be three armed park rangers with you at all times for the remainder of your hike on the Appalachian Trail. All three will stand guard while you are sleeping so nothing even remotely close to this nightmare can happen again. I have arranged for each of you to contact your wives. I want you to speak with them before we decide whether or not to proceed. We will do this as quickly as possible. I have four private rooms available for you and you each have twenty minutes to talk with them. Come with me now and I will lead you to your rooms."

We followed Ron, I took the first room and made the call to Susan.

"Hello" she answered.

"Hey! How's it going?" I asked a little over enthusiastically.

"Thank God you are okay. I have been praying for you ever since I got the call this morning. Tell me what happened."

I spent the next five minutes giving her the details of our horrific night. I could hear her crying on the other end.

"Susan, I need for you to pull yourself together. I promise you that I am fine. Ron has arranged for three park rangers to be with us for the rest of the trip. And we will be off the trail in a day and a half. I assure you that I will be perfectly safe. But you have to be fine with it for me to continue."

"I was just so scared" she said between sobs. "I was afraid that I was going to lose you. The whole thing is just so unbelievable."

"I know sweetie. I was scared too. I am still pretty freaked out about the whole thing. Tell me what you think."

"If you say that you are safe then I believe you."

"So you are okay with me going on?"

"Yeah. I just miss you so much. Just get off that damn trail as fast as you can."

"I will. And I miss you too. I love you."

"I love you too. Do you want to talk to Thomas?" she asked.

"Of course"

"Okay, here he is. It's Da Da."

"Hi Thomas. How are you doing buddy" I said in a voice only reserved for him.

"Da Da. Da Da" he replied. Those were the greatest words that I could hear. But they also made me a little sad. I really missed my family.

Susan got back on the phone. "I bet you are glad to hear his voice."

THE ULTIMATE CHALLENGE

"And yours. Is he doing anything new?"

"Oh yeah. He is really into trucks. Whenever he sees one, he points it out. He is also spinning around until he gets dizzy and falls down."

"How are you making it?" I asked.

"I'm fine. I watch you a lot. You guys are the hottest thing going. Every time that I watch something else it's The Ultimate Challenge this and The Ultimate Challenge that. It is crazy."

"Well, I have to go. I miss and love you."

"I love you to. Be careful."

We returned to the break room at about the same time to see Mr. Craig. I was in great spirits. Susan and Thomas lifted me up like they always do. I don't know what I did to deserve such a beautiful family but I am truly blessed. We all took seats and faced the attorney.

"So what is the verdict?" he asked.

"I'm ready to go" I said.

"Same here" Eric replied.

"I'm good to go" Drew answered.

That left Jason. He sat speechless, staring at his empty cup of coffee.

"Jason, what about you?" Ron asked.

"I'm done" he replied.

"What? You're done? You're not done" Eric screamed.

"Yes, I am done" Jason quietly answered.

"You mean that you are just going to quit. You are just going to ruin this for all of us" Drew angrily stated.

"I'm sorry guys. I just can't take it anymore. And Kim…"

"It's her isn't it" Eric said. "You have got to be kidding me. When are you going to start doing what you want to do? We have a chance to change our lives and our family's lives. Do you have any clue how fortunate we are? And now you are going to blow it for all of us. Where is your competitiveness? Where is your dignity and where in the world is your heart?"

Jason's eyes filled with tears of anger and sorrow. "I'm really sorry. But I am going to spend the rest of my life with Kim. She is my wife and my loyalty is with her. Plus a guy is dead and we were almost killed ourselves. And you guys are brushing it off like nothing happened. A guy is dead! You can call me a wimp. You can call me whatever you want. I really don't care."

Drew was the best fence mender of the group. He was by far the most compassionate member of our team and now he was our only hope.

"Jason, none of us wanted this to happen. But whether we quit or not, Earl is still dead. We can't change that but it wasn't our fault. And believe me, we all know that your ultimate loyalty is to your wife. You are the most loyal person that I have ever met. So we understand how important Kim's opinion is to you. But we have got to see this thing through. If we quit now, we will all spend the rest of our lives wondering what if? And that includes you. You know that is true Jason. Do you want to live that way?"

"No. Not really."

THE ULTIMATE CHALLENGE

"So call her back. Tell her you love her. And if she loves you, she has to let you do this. You have to do this for yourself, not us."

"You're right. I need to finish this. I feel like I have never finished anything in my life" Jason answered with tears still streaming down his face.

This was the first time that I had ever seen Jason cry. And we had been friends since Little League baseball. As I watched him, I felt tears welling up in my eyes but I tried to hide it. I also felt guilty for yelling at him. I had been way out of line and I knew it. This was only the third time that I had ever had real conflict with him. He was the most mild mannered, even tempered guy that I had ever met. We had gotten into one argument in seventeen years and two during the past seven hours. I would make peace with him eventually.

Thank God that Drew was back to himself. He was no longer the insane lunatic, but his usual caring self. Drew was also the greatest salesman that I had ever met. He had just taken a situation that seemed impossible and completely turned the tables within minutes. He had a special gift of delivering his point of view in a way that always seemed appealing to others. It came naturally to him and he almost always got his way because in his mind, there was no other way. Without Drew, we would be packing our bags and heading home. Because of Drew, we were more determined than ever to win The Ultimate Challenge.

Chapter 17

Ron told us that he would make a brief statement to the press while we escaped from the back of the building on the four wheelers with the park rangers. Before we knew it, we were on our way to finish our stint on the dangerous Appalachian Trail. We arrived back at our campsite at 9:00 A.M. Three park rangers were waiting for us there and we also had a new cameraman. The park rangers did us a favor by packing up our belongings so minutes after we arrived, we were ready to go. Poor Earl's tent still remained with police tape wrapped around the perimeter. It was a dim reminder of the previous night's tragedy.

We covered eighteen miles that day, stopping only twice to catch our breath. Once again we were behind. We wanted to get as far away from the last night's campsite as possible. For that matter, we wanted to get as far away from the Appalachian Trail as possible. As darkness was setting in we found a place to camp. We knew that we would finish our hike tomorrow which brought a renewed sense of energy and anticipation to our team. Things were different now though because you can't immediately erase a tragedy like the one that had happened. It was comforting to have three more people in our camp. That would allow us to sleep without fear.

Dinner was dehydrated chicken and vegetables, another crappy meal. We had eaten all the good stuff on our first half of the hike. I don't know why we did it, but we did. Now everything left was just something that we ate to get some energy. We were all exhausted. The hike had really torn us down physically.

Combining the physical toll with the emotional strain and lack of sleep the previous night made us slugs. It made us feel as though we had lived a lifetime in the last four days.

The conversation was minimal.

Eric asked "Do you think they made it out today?"

"No way" Drew responded. "They only had two and a half hours on us. And we were ahead of them last night."

"How is Barbara?" I asked.

"She's all right. Her morning sickness is getting better, but she is gaining quite a bit of weight. She is all worried about it. I told her, you're supposed to gain weight when you are pregnant."

From there the conversation died and we all turned in early in an attempt to sleep off our depression. Jason and I slept inches apart without saying a word to each other. I tossed and turned for an hour, no doubt keeping Jason awake also. When I did finally dose off, the sleep was very deep. I woke up to my own scream in the middle of the night. It was just a dream but the murderer was coming after me. I knew that it was just a dream but it kind of freaked me out anyway so I quietly crawled to the front of the tent, unzipped the zipper half way and poked my head out. The park rangers were in place, our own personal body guards.

The cold air against my face woke me up, so I laid back down and rehashed the previous day's events. I couldn't get my mind off of Earl the cameraman. We learned that he was married with a seven year old daughter. Our team had already decided that if we won, Earl's family would receive a sizeable donation from each of us. Within half an hour everyone was stirring, no one could sleep any longer. It was 4:00 A.M. and we didn't want to wait around so we packed up and started the final leg led by our flashlights. The park rangers were glad to

THE ULTIMATE CHALLENGE

leave early because the sooner that we left, the sooner their job would be done. We were eager to finish the race and very eager to hopefully catch Team Nike. We hiked as fast as we could with the lure of the finish line providing the energy boost that we needed.

We entered Team Nike's camp at 5:30 A.M. It was still dark out and we eased by their camp as quietly as we could. The park rangers guarding Team Nike cooperated and the loud snores coming from the tent drowned out the sounds of the crackling leaves as we passed. We were once again in the lead with no plans to relinquish it. The crack of dawn brought us a new cameraman and the realization that we had only five miles to go. If the rednecks had any sense at all, they would realize that we had passed them when they found only one cameraman waiting at the five mile mark. We didn't even wait for our new cameraman to get going, he had to catch up to us. We sensed the end of our hike and wanted to expand our lead.

The final stretch was easy as far as the Appalachian Trail goes. We were hiking along a ridge so we were on flat ground which allowed us to walk briskly. With half a mile to go, we could see the finish line. Ron Craig was waiting for us as well as television crews from all around the country. Almost one thousand people came to watch us finish one leg of the race and start another. As we crossed the finish line, a huge weight was lifted off of our shoulders. We all made a pact on the hike that everything that happened on the Appalachian Trail when we were not being filmed would stay on the Appalachian Trail. Unfortunately for Drew, most of it was caught on film by the night cameras that Earl had set up. The end of our hike was a new start for us. We knew that many challenges still awaited us, but we could not imagine a scenario that was more physically and mentally as grueling as this one.

Ron greeted us with a smile and we talked while we walked. "Guys, you just finished the leg that is probably the most physically exhausting part of the challenge. Your instructions are on CD in the RV just like last time. If everything is all right, I will leave you alone."

"How is the serial killer?" I asked.

"He is fine. He is going to spend a few nights in the hospital under tight security and then he will be transferred to the Federal Penitentiary in Atlanta. Now that the FBI has him, they are not going to let him go."

Park rangers and policemen blocked off a pathway for us from the trail to the RV. We waved at the fans as we made our way. It was nice to be around people again. A groups of reporters were stationed around the RV and they all screamed questions at us as we passed.

"How does it feel to shoot someone?"

"Do you think that you could have prevented the murder if you had acted faster?"

"What do you have to say to Earl Jones' widow?"

The reporters wanted something, anything from us. Ron had advised us not to say anything about the incident publicly and we were happy to oblige. But the questions hit me hard. They were brutal. The answers wouldn't come to me today, if ever. The Ultimate Challenge was truly that. We were challenged in ways that we never deemed possible. This race would now always be tainted in our minds. Whoever said that fame and fortune comes with a price was right. We would always have to live with Earl Jones' death in our minds. What happens on the AT stays on the AT was a pact that was much easier said than done.

Chapter 18

The RV was a beautiful thing to see. Cushy seats, plenty of food and even a bed to stretch out on. We quickly crowded into the small back bedroom and turned on the CD player to see where we were going next. Once again, John Simmons popped up on the screen.

"Hey guys. I bet that you are worn out." We all exchanged glances that said, if you only knew. He continued "The purpose of this race isn't to kill you so now you are going to do something fun. Your next destination is the Windy City. You are going to Chicago. Wrigley Field to be specific. Have you ever wanted to take batting practice in a Major League ballpark? Well now is your chance. Your next challenge is that one team member must hit a homerun at Wrigley Field. A pitching machine will be set up and each team member will take ten swings. You will continue rotating until someone hits a homerun. Oh, and one more thing, there is going to be a crowd. Every fan that shows up to watch you gets a free ticket to a Cubs game. Have fun."

I was so excited. I looked at Jason and he was grinning from ear to ear. I had never been to Wrigley Field but I loved it anyway. Wrigley was one of the last great old ballparks still in existence. I grew up watching the Cubs on WGN. They have not won a World Series in decades but faithful Cubs fans still flock to Wrigley Field year after year. Eric climbed behind the wheel and we were on our way. Drew and I lounged on the bed in the back of the RV.

"You know, I bet John had a blast planning this thing" Drew said.

"I know he did" I answered. "If you combine his creative imagination with an unlimited budget, there is no telling what he has dreamed up for us to do."

"But why Chicago?" Drew asked.

"You have to remember that John was a huge sports history buff, so there were really only two choices. It was either Wrigley Field or Fenway Park in Boston. Those are the only great old ballparks that are left."

"I haven't hit a baseball in fifteen years" Drew said.

"It is not going to be easy. But it is a heck of a lot better than hiking. And we have one advantage because of my now former career. I spent a lot of time around baseball coaches and I have learned so much about how to hit a baseball a long way."

"It is better than hiking."

Jason was navigating for Eric, so Drew and I took a nice long nap. The bed felt so good. I curled up under the covers and joked to Drew "wake me up when we get there."

We arrived in Knoxville, Tennessee at 9:00 AM. Our drive would take us through Lexington, Kentucky, Cincinnati Ohio, Indianapolis and then up to Chicago. The trip was five hundred fifty miles so without any major problems we hoped to be swinging the bat by 4:00 central time. We decided to drive in two hour stints to keep everyone fresh. I was going to drive last so I took full advantage and slept for five hours. I didn't hear a thing. I didn't know when we pulled over to switch drivers, it was great and I needed it very badly. Eric woke me up when we were almost to Indianapolis.

"Holland, you are driving in an hour."

THE ULTIMATE CHALLENGE

""Are we making good time?"

"Yeah, we just filled the tank up and picked up some burgers so you can eat before it is your turn to drive."

"Thanks man. I am hungry."

They had gotten me a Big Mac meal. I hadn't eaten junk food in over two months so this was a real treat. I savored every bite of my two all-beef patties, special sauce lettuce cheese pickles onion on a sesame seed bun. The fries were great too. But the Coke was almost undrinkable. The break from soft drinks had really taken its toll. With all of that sugar, how did I ever drink these things? After taking three sips, I opted for a bottled water out of the fridge.

Drew was driving so I went up front to talk to him and keep him awake.

"How are you doing?"

"Pretty good" Drew answered.

"I slept like a baby on that bed."

We were now in Indianapolis and passing the famous Indianapolis 500 speedway. It was nice to be indoors for a change. If you are cold all that you have to do is press a button to warm up. It was also very nice to sit in a cushioned seat. After sleeping on the hard ground for several nights, the RV was a nice respite.

Before I took my nap, I had turned the cell phone on ringer and left it in the front of the RV. The phone rang just as we were leaving Indianapolis. I answered it and as usual Ron Craig was on the other end.

"Hey Mark, how are you guys doing?"

"What's wrong now?" I asked.

"Nothing is wrong. I just want to let you know that we are going to be tightening security. Two FBI agents out of Indianapolis are going to be following you for a couple of days."

"FBI! What's going on Ron? And I want the truth!"

"Okay. We have a little problem, but it is nothing for you guys to worry about" Ron explained.

"What is it? Tell me now!"

"John Albert Henley is missing. He jumped out of a third story window at the hospital and no one can find him."

"Oh my lord" I exclaimed.

Drew was taking his eyes off of the road "What is it? What's wrong?"

I waved my hands at him to tell him to be quiet.

Ron continued "The FBI has a major manhunt underway. They only want to protect you as a precaution. Remember Mark, this guy has been badly injured. He is looking for a place to hide. The last thing on his mind is revenge."

"That is easy for you to say" I said before hanging up the phone.

Jason and Eric heard the commotion and had crowded into the front cabin to listen.

"Well guys, John Albert Henley has escaped from the hospital and the FBI is tailing us as a precaution."

THE ULTIMATE CHALLENGE

"No way" Drew said.

"When is this crap going to end?" Eric asked.

Jason put his face in his hands and took refuge in the back room without saying a word.

"He is hurt bad. There is no way that he comes after us" I said while trying to reassure my friends.

"You don't know that. You shot him and Drew peed in his face. If that was me, I would be coming after you" Eric said.

"He's just lucky that I didn't have to take a dump" Drew said in an attempt to add a little humor to the situation.

"Man, you are crazy! How can you joke about this?" Eric asked.

"He is not going to come after us" Drew replied.

A two minute phone conversation had changed everything. Every car that we passed was now suspicious. We noticed a new sedan following us, no doubt our new friends from the FBI. Our guard was up and the small talk stopped.

"I'm going to pull over and let you drive."

We switched places quickly and I got the RV up to seventy miles an hour which was as fast as it would let me go. John Simmons did not plan this. He wanted us to be worried about Team Nike, not a crazy serial killer. My mind was working as we drove and I decided to call Ron Craig.

"Ron, its Mark. Does the television audience know that we are headed to Wrigley Field?"

"Yes they do Mark. The camera was rolling when you watched the video tape."

"So he could be on his way here."

"No way Mark. He can barely walk, much less drive."

"Ron, he eluded law enforcement for five years and lived off of the land. He is no ordinary guy."

Ron responded "He doesn't like crowds Mark. Think about it, he has been hiding in one of the most remote places in the country. We have doubled security at Wrigley Field. The guys knows that he is caught if he goes anywhere near there."

"If he wants us, he will find us. I want another gun."

"You are overreacting Mark."

I once again hung the phone up on Ron. We made our way through the farmland of northern Indiana and southern Illinois. The closer that we got to Chicago the more buildings that we saw. There was no room for grass. It was business after business or house after house. It was not a great place for someone that needs their space. I was wondering why in the world anyone would want to live there when all of a sudden the most incredible skyline that I had ever seen popped into view. Downtown Chicago was huge! And the buildings each had their own unique style making the view even more beautiful. I came to the conclusion that in Chicago, downtown was the very best place to live.

Our timing was just right because we barely missed rush hour traffic. We found Wrigley Field fairly easily and the hair on my arms stood straight up when I caught my first glimpse of the majestic ballpark. I decided in my mind to forget about John Albert Henley and enjoy this magical experience that John

THE ULTIMATE CHALLENGE

Simmons had planned for us. As we drove up to the ballpark, we could see that the Chicago Cubs had gone to great lengths to make this event a success. Vendors were out in full force and the electronic sign in front of the ballpark said "The Chicago Cubs welcome The Ultimate Challenge to Wrigley Field." Cubs fans were everywhere and they cheered at our arrival when they saw the RV. Not only was every fan in attendance given a free ticket to a Cubs game but concessions were only one dollar each. A local radio station was working the event along with WGN.

Event security directed us to the player's parking lot and as soon as we parked we were out of the RV and ready to go. As we walked onto the field, I stopped for a second and looked all around the park in awe. The green ivy in the outfield was starting to bloom but you could still see the all brick outfield. I looked up to the buildings on Waveland Avenue that overlooked the ballpark. As usual, people were hanging out of the rooftops of the buildings to examine The Ultimate Challenge from afar. The crowd was decent, several thousand people had come to cheer us on. But the ballpark looked empty. Fans were seated between first and third base on the field level but the rest of the stadium was vacant. Everyone in attendance had a great seat. I looked up at the flag and the wind was blowing out to right field which was great for Jason and I because we were both lefties.

The field was immaculate, the proud baby of a full time grounds crew. The grass was perfectly manicured, so clean and cut so fine that you could eat off of it. The dirt around the base paths had been dragged and raked, then dragged again. The field crew had lined the first and third base lines with chalk and also the batter's box. They had even put the bases out even though we wouldn't be running. The grounds crew had done a terrific job, using the same routine that they used before a real game.

Music was blaring from the loudspeakers as we made our way towards home plate. We waved to the crowd as we walked. I stared at the press boxes, trying to imagine which one had housed the late great Harry Carey. I grew up listening to him announce the games and sing "Take me out to the ballgame" during the seventh inning stretch. Harry was a legend and his greatness only added to the mystique of Wrigley Field.

The ballpark had always been my safe haven. For my entire life, if something went wrong I would go to the ballpark. It didn't matter what ballpark, just as long as baseball was being played. The ballpark is the perfect place to forget about your worries and leave your troubles behind if only for a few hours.

Wrigley field is the ultimate ballpark to go to because when you walk in, you are taken fifty years back in time. It allows you to revert back to the past for a few hours. It doesn't have the comfortable amenities of the new ballparks and it is even showing its age somewhat. But fans like that, it is what draws baseball fans from all over the country to visit. I glanced at Jason and he was enjoying the moment every bit as much as I was. Jason loved baseball in the same way that I did so this was as big a thrill for him as it was for me.

As we approached home plate, the first task was to pick our weapon. Luckily for us, we were allowed to use aluminum bats, which would allow us to hit the ball much further than wood bats would allow. We needed every advantage that we could get. I chose a Worth composite bat. In my opinion Worth bats were far superior to their competitors.

Jason was going to hit first. He easily had the best swing out of the four of us. Jason's swing was a textbook left handed swing but he was more of a line drive hitter than power hitter. He would be swinging for the fences today though. I was always a pitcher but I had a little bit of power. Drew was pretty good at anything he tried so he had a decent swing but it was rusty. Eric was another story all together. He was by far the strongest member of our group but he couldn't swing a baseball bat to save his life. And it killed him. Eric's philosophy is, the stronger you are the farther the ball should go. He did not really realize that there is a real art to hitting a baseball. Hand-eye coordination, rhythm, timing, major use of the entire core of your body and keeping your

THE ULTIMATE CHALLENGE

hands inside of the ball all played important roles in hitting a baseball. Strength didn't hurt but without everything else, it didn't really matter how much you could bench press.

In my humble opinion, hitting a baseball is the hardest single thing that you can do in sports. A nine inch ball is traveling towards you sometimes in excess of ninety miles an hour. The ball may drop, curve or move in any direction when it is approaching. You have to decide whether to swing or not in a fraction of a second. Baseball is a game of strategy and that is why so many people in today's world can't appreciate it. Today's crowd could have cared less about strategy or action because they all got a free ticket to a Cubs game and beer was half price.

As we warmed up to hit, we received a great surprise because Mr. Cub himself, Ernie Banks, came out to get the festivities underway. Banks said a few words then introduced us and Jason stepped up to the plate. As I nervously stared at my friend, I realized that our dream was coming true. When we were little we always dreamed of playing in a Major League ballpark. Now he was standing in the same batter's box where so many great professional baseball players had stood. It was unbelievable.

Jason took the first pitch that came to him. He swung and missed the second, drawing boos from the drunken crowd. He lined the third pitch to right field and the crowd was back on his side. Jason hit the ball well but didn't come close to hitting a homerun. He left the batter's box grinning and shaking his head.

Eric jumped into the box next, taking a wild practice swing. He rocked back and forth from his left foot to his right and he waited for the first pitch to arrive. As the ball approached him, he generated a mighty swing, grunting as he swung the bat. He missed the ball by three feet and his momentum spun him completely around. He then lost his balance and fell to the ground. Eric's all or nothing swing immediately made him a crowd favorite. The crowd cheered wildly as Eric picked himself up off of the ground, dusted off his Reebok warm up suit and waved to the fans. Eric swung and missed the next eight balls. Then he stepped out of the box to regain his composure before the tenth and final pitch. The crowd was on their feet cheering as he once again swung the bat with all of his might. The ping of the aluminum bat that he was using echoed throughout the ballpark as the crowd hushed in anticipation of where his powerful swing would take the ball. The ball traveled a mile into the sky before reaching its peak and ultimate destination, thirty feet in front of home plate. Eric played with the crowd by bowing to them and they responded kindly.

Drew hit next. I stood next to Jason as we watched him dig into the batter's box.

Chapter 19

The shots were fired from the outfield bleachers. My first thought was that someone had set off firecrackers inside of the stadium. Jason and I were focusing on Drew when we heard the pop and then almost simultaneously saw him drop his bat. The second shot landed directly behind us because we heard a thump against the brick wall to our backs.

I immediately made a quick path to the dugout by taking three steps and then diving into the sunken hole. Jason and Eric were right behind me. We all rolled down the dugout steps and laid flat on the floor. I then curled up into the fetal position and prayed.

Drew was not so lucky. He was still at home plate in the middle of the field. When he realized what was happening, he turned toward one dugout and then the other. He was a deer in the headlights, frozen in fear. He decided that he could not make it to the shelter so he hit the ground and covered his head with his hands.

The crowd responded to our actions and panic quickly set in. Sick screams of fear resounded throughout the park. Some fans were dashing to the exits. Total mayhem ensued as slower fans were simply run over. Others were jumping through rows of seats, unwilling to wait for the aisles to clear. Others simply laid on the ground, letting the seats in front of them serve as a shield for the spray of bullets.

The stadium was mostly empty, so the echoes made it difficult to determine exactly where the bullets had come from. Unbeknown to us, the FBI had sharpshooters positioned on the roof of Wrigley Field. One of the agents finally spotted the shooter, who was located just beyond the left field bleachers. The gunfire from the sharpshooter set off a second round of fear. The screams escalated as the fans feared for their lives. The second round of gunfire terrified me again also as I squeezed my closed eyes even tighter.

Then an awkward silence ensued as we all waited for more gunfire. But none was there. An FBI agent disguised as Wrigley Field security ran over to Drew as another agent approached us.

"We got him" the agent said as he approached. "You can get up now. The shooter is dead."

"Are you sure? Jason asked, still curled up in a ball.

"I am sure. You are fine now."

"Is it John Albert Henley?" I asked.

"We are not sure, but we think so.

Drew screamed hysterically as the agent approached him. He was definitely on the verge of a breakdown.

As security guards gained control of the small crowd, more information started coming in. The gunman was the serial killer that had been stalking us. Our worst fear had become reality. The FBI had monitored every flight out of Atlanta to Chicago. But Henley had once again eluded law enforcement by cleaning up, driving to Nashville, flying to St. Louis and then to Chicago. In the back of my mind, I really was not surprised that he had come after us. If he wanted to make a statement, we were the perfect targets because we had a national television audience. Plus, we had caught him. And Drew peed on him. No one likes getting peed on.

Wrigley Field security opened the Cubs clubhouse for us to rest in. Drew had to be escorted in. His hands were shaking. He had just stared death straight in the face.

Ron called us on the speaker phone in the Cubs clubhouse. "Is everyone OK?" he asked.

"We are fine. Just a little shook up" I replied.

"I don't know what to say to you guys. I feel terrible. I am doing everything that I can to protect you."

"Ron, it is not your fault. If the FBI had not been here, we could all probably be dead right now."

"To be perfectly honest, I am a little relieved" Jason surprisingly said. That was a strong comment coming from Jason and it helped us all to calm down.

"I just hope that you guys can try in some way to put this behind you and eventually enjoy this race again. I realize that is probably going to be impossible now. But you don't deserve this and John Simmons would never have dreamed of putting you in harm's way."

"We are going to be fine, Ron" Eric answered.

We hung up the phone, had a team meeting and after an hour of deliberations decided that we would continue the race. It was my turn to hit and when we went back on the field the only people that were left were FBI officials, local policemen and Wrigley Field employees. Every news truck in the city of Chicago was camped outside of Wrigley, demanding entrance into the park. The bat that Drew had been using was now evidence because a bullet had pierced the aluminum and was now stuck in the bat. The bat had saved Drew's life. I grabbed a composite Worth bat and began my way to the plate.

We all glanced around nervously, knowing that the gunman was dead, but still unsure of anything. Drew looked pale and sickly. He had barely escaped one attack on the hiking trail and the second near death experience was just about more than he could handle. He was at his wits end and it was incredible that he even agreed to continue the race.

Just as I was beginning to take my warm up swings, Team Nike sprinted onto the field, running towards home plate. I knew by the look on the redneck's faces that we were about to have a problem. I stood in the batter's box and watched them approach us.

"Ronnie, the head red neck, entered the right side of the batter's box and said "Get out of here. It's our turn to hit."

"No, it is not your turn to hit. I am not moving."

"If you queers haven't hit a homerun by now, you're not going to so get out of my way." Ronnie then took a step towards me. I tightened my grip on the bat in my hands, ready to defend myself.

"First of all" I said. "You are going to get out of my face! Second, we are going to call Ron Craig. And last, I am going to give you a warning. If you redneck hicks mess with us today, I am going to take this bat and pound your skull until I see grey matter on home plate. I am about to snap and if we fight, one of us isn't going to leave here alive. That is a promise."

"Get Ron on the phone" Ronnie demanded as he continued staring into my eyes. We made a conference call to Ron and he explained that our team could finish our round of hitting. Then team Nike would hit for a round and we

THE ULTIMATE CHALLENGE

would rotate for as long as needed. Ronnie backed off of the plate and joined his teammates in the on deck circle. They all picked Easton bats which didn't surprise me at all.

My teammates were shouting words of encouragement, but I heard nothing. Wrigley Field could have been full of fans and I would not have heard a thing. I was angry and in a zone, an unexplained phenomena where I was channeling all of my emotions to do one thing. The anger, excitement and anticipation raised my adrenaline level to the point where I felt unbeatable. My body was completely numb.

I tapped my right foot with the bat and my left cleat dug into the dirt to anchor my weight. I lifted the bat up off of my shoulder and then back. My bat laid still, waiting for the pitch to come. As the ball made its way from the pitching machine to the plate I cocked the bat ever so slightly. My arms started first, quickly followed by my hips. My downswing made perfect contact with the lower half of the ball. I did not feel a thing as the bat made contact with the ball which was the greatest feeling that a hitter could have. I watched the ball hit the barrel and followed through the contact for as long as I could. The ball was traveling high in the air, flying directly down the right field line. I had gotten all of it. A miracle then happened as the famous Wrigley Field wind took the ball not only over the fence but into the bleachers. I was outwardly calm but on the inside I was jumping for joy. I glared at the rednecks, dropped my bat on home plate and began our walk towards the vehicle.

Jason caught up to me as we walked down the left field line on our way to the player's parking lot. Jason and I had not spoken much since Earl's death.

"So how did it feel?"

I looked at Jason and couldn't stop grinning. "It was awesome. Can you believe all of this crap?

"No, yes, I don't know. The world could come to an end right now and it would not surprise me."

"Drew has got to be freaked out right now" I said.

"If the bullet goes one inch in either direction, he is dead" Jason answered.

"Do you think we can put this behind us?" I asked.

"For the rest of this race? Oh yes. But in ten years, we will all definitely be in therapy. At least Henley is dead now." Jason said.

"I am a little surprised to hear you say that."

"Hey man, he was coming after us. I may be sympathetic, but everyone has their limits. If someone wants me dead I am looking out for number one."

"The way that I see it is he killed Earl and tried to kill us and he had never met any of us. The whole serial killer on the loose thing makes it easier to get over too. At least another innocent person didn't die."

" I just want to win this race" Jason answered. "Nobody is after us now so we can just focus, have fun and hopefully win a lot of money at the end of this thing."

Before we exited the ballpark, we took one last look at Wrigley Field. We arrived at Wrigley so excited and we left just happy to be alive.

We climbed into the RV and were thankful that security had cleared a path for us to get through the mob of reporters. We pushed play once again on the DVR to learn about our next challenge. John Simmons appeared on the screen. I was so glad that he wasn't here to see everything that had gone wrong with the race that he was so excited about.

Chapter 20

"Hey guys. That challenge was for all of you guys but especially for Jason and Mark. I really hope that you enjoyed it and enjoyed Wrigley Field. I know that all of you are probably pretty exhausted, so you are about to begin a twelve hour mandatory rest period. Tonight you all will be staying in a luxury suite in downtown Chicago. You will find directions on your dashboard. The twelve hour rest begins when you open the door to your room. Have a great night and enjoy the view."

Eric drove as I opened the blinds to my window to enjoy the short trip. It was dark outside now and when the bright lights of downtown Chicago appeared, I understood why so many movies had been made there. I had never seen a downtown landscape that was so beautiful at night. The entire skyline was filled for miles with buildings of all shapes and sizes. It looked more like a postcard than a reality. After a thirty minute drive we reached our destination. It was 8:00 P.M. and we were famished. Lunch was long gone.

The bell-hop greeted us at the door and told us that we would be staying on the 52nd floor. The elevator took us to our floor at incredible speed. Our suite was amazing. We had an incredible view of downtown. One entire wall of our suite was nothing but windows. We all made our way directly to the scenic view while ignoring the plush accommodations. We had a wonderful view of the historic Wrigley building. We also had a great view of the river that travels right through the middle of downtown Chicago. The downtown landscape was the perfect mixture of historic old buildings and new unique towers.

After spending ten minutes admiring the view, our hunger took over. Dinner was provided for us, it was Johnny's Italian Beef sandwiches. The hotel employee that delivered the sandwiches to us said that they were John Simmons favorite. He said that Johnny's is an independently owned sandwich stand and they have the best Italian beef sandwich in all of Chicago. He said that locals stood in long lines at all times of the year to get them. I had never heard of Italian beef but was certainly willing to try it.

The Italian beef is cut paper thin and marinated in its own juice for hours after it is cooked. It is topped with sweet peppers and placed in fresh bread that melts in your mouth. The sandwich is then dipped in juice which makes eating it a messy endeavor. After one bite of the sandwich, I was in love. At the time, I would place the sandwich as number one on my list of favorite foods. I savored every incredible bite and devoured two full foot long sandwiches. I would have attempted to eat a third if my stomach would have allowed it.

Jason and Eric turned in early because they did not have the benefit of the nap that Drew and I had enjoyed. We turned off the lights in the living area and sat in the dark, staring at the Chicago skyline.

"I should be dead right now" Drew said after five minutes of silence.

"You are very fortunate" I answered. "The man upstairs was with you today."

"I have never believed in the man upstairs. You know that."

"You really don't believe that there is a God?" I asked.

"Honestly, I don't know what I believe. I have never seen or felt anything in my life to prove to me that there is a God. So what makes you so sure?"

THE ULTIMATE CHALLENGE

"Hey man, I wrestle with it also. I have been lucky enough to see a lot of this country and it is hard for me to believe that it was all created by accident. I have seen too many beautiful things to believe that they were just randomly made by a big explosion. And when Thomas was born, I was sure of it. It was such an amazing thing."

Drew's interest was sparked "But what makes you sure?"

"Drew, you are a realist just like me. So that makes the entire subject pretty difficult. You believe in things that you can see and hear. I totally get it and respect that. I would be totally lying to you if I said that I have never doubted whether God is real. I guess it boils down to one word, faith."

"Faith in what?"

"Faith that there is a higher power that watches over me and my family. Faith that when I die, that there is a better place that I will go. I know that it sounds crazy to a realist, but I totally believe in angels. When I look back at my life and think of the stupid, crazy things that could have and probably should have killed me, I can't help but think that angels were watching over me."

"What about innocent people like Earl that was just doing his job? And what about all of the starving babies around the world? And what about cavemen and dinosaurs?"

"I have asked myself all of those questions. And I don't pretend to know all of the answers. I think that anyone that pretends to know all of the answers is full of it. Why did I live after putting myself in bad situations? Why was I so special? Why do people get cancer? And why do some people with cancer die and other people live? Some things, I just don't understand. But at the end of the day, I just believe in God. It is not any one thing in particular."

Drew looked out over the lights of the wonderful skyline. "I hear what you are saying. And I want to believe in God, but I see all of the crazy stuff in the news and on television and it seems to me like all of those people really just want money. Some of them seem so fake. It's like, if you give them money you shall be healed. And if you don't believe exactly like I do, you will go to hell."

"I get it and I'm with you there. You have these extremist right wing people claiming to be Christians that really turn people off. And they argue with radical atheists that are just as closed minded as the radical Christians. And with media outlets, you are going to hear about the radical stuff a lot more than normal stuff. That is just what our world has turned into. There is a great divide, kind of a line drawn in the sand with radical people on both sides of the line. But I think that there are millions of people standing on that line. People that won't really alienate other people for thinking something different than they do."

"It is a tough conversation with a lot more questions than answers."

"Yes it is. Always remember that it is your journey. That is the great thing about faith. It is your journey. So many people are influenced by others. Don't be one of those people. It is okay to have questions and doubt and not get all of the answers. I truly believe that generalizing any group is very lazy. It is taking the easy way out."

Drew looked more confused than when we started talking. "I'm not sure what I believe but if God is real, I think that he might have saved my life today."

"We better go to bed" I said. It was getting late and we needed our rest. After such a traumatic day, it was nice to sleep in an actual bed. The bed in the RV was nice but nothing like the soothing comfort that a real bed provided. Nonetheless, I had a hard time getting to sleep. The harder I tried, the worse it got. I just couldn't get the shooting out of my mind. I had never been shot at before. I spent an hour and a half trying to fight off panic attacks in the moments just before sleep. I would almost fall to sleep and then feel a jolt in my chest and

THE ULTIMATE CHALLENGE

I couldn't make it go away. When I finally did fall asleep for good, I slept hard without even a hint of a dream about John Albert Henley.

I was woken up at 7:00 A.M. by a knock on the door. It was breakfast and it was wonderful. Eggs, bacon, biscuits, hash browns and pancakes with maple syrup. After eating, I made my way once again to the wall of windows. The river was green and went right beside our window. To the left was a park that led up to the Buckingham Fountain. In front of it was the Museum of Fine Arts which housed some of the most famous paintings in the world. If you got right up next to the window and looked to the left, you could barely see Soldier Field, the historic home of the Chicago Bears. And to my surprise, directly below us was a par three golf course. A golf course in the middle of downtown Chicago just seemed so out of place. Our twelve hour break was almost over so we took showers and prepared for our exit.

Chapter 21

Our RV was waiting for us downstairs. It had been filled with gas so we were ready to go. Our instructions were written for us on a piece of paper attached to the steering wheel. We were to drive to Midway airport where we would catch John Simmons private plane to Las Vegas. Drew and Jason had been to Vegas and loved it. I, on the other hand, had never had the desire to go.

A pilot was waiting for us as the directions took us directly to the hanger where our private plane was waiting. I was wondering what kind of challenge could possibly be waiting for us in Las Vegas. It seemed more like a vacation spot than an adventure waiting to happen.

John's plane was first class from top to bottom. We sat in reclining leather seats, treated ourselves to a full snack bar and watched "Raising Arizona" on a pull down movie screen. The cabin of the aircraft felt more like a living room than an airplane. You could stretch your legs as far as they would go, you could eat or drink whatever you wanted and the bathroom was about two times bigger than any commercial flight that I had ever been on.

"This is the life" Eric said to me.

"If we win, this could be our life. What are your plans if you win?" I asked.

"First, I am going to take a year off. I will just work out and enjoy everything. Then I am going to try to be a volunteer assistant coach at a Division One college football program. Either Tennessee or Georgia."

"I knew that you would still want to coach." I said.

"Yeah, it is in my blood. I love it. I love practice, I love watching film and I really love game day."

"How was your phone call to Jessica?"

"She said that she was worried about me. I don't know if I believe her though. I just hope that I didn't make a mistake in getting married. Something just doesn't feel right."

"Can you imagine living without her?"

"Maybe. Yes. I don't know."

"Do you love her?"

"Yeah I love her. I am starting to miss her a little bit. I never thought I would say that. It's just not what I thought it would be, you know?"

"Not really. But I do know that marriage is hard work. You have to give a little and take a little. You're going to be all right. If you take a year off, you can go places with her and spend a lot of quality time together."

We landed at 11:30 A.M. Las Vegas time. A limo picked us up at the terminal and we were off. The way that the town was built seemed very odd to me. In the middle of a barren desert were all of these beautiful hotels. It was a town surrounded by nothing. We drove down the strip and the only thing that I could think of was how much money had been spent here. Las Vegas is like

THE ULTIMATE CHALLENGE

an adult Disney World. These people had built a dream world with budget as no concern. I recognized most of the hotel names. The Mirage, Caesar's Palace. One hotel had a roller coaster on top of it and another was designed to replicate Paris, France.

The taxi pulled up to our hotel The Venetian. It was pretty amazing. The ceilings on the entryway in the front of the hotel were painted like the Sistine Chapel. It must have taken years to do. Inside, the hotel was overwhelming. To get almost anywhere, you had to go through the casino, a genius design by the builders. The casino was nice but smelled like smoke. Slot machines were ringing and jingling on one side with blackjack and craps tables on the other side. Our personal escort from the hotel was leading us to our rooms. We passed the blackjack tables and three of the tables had one hundred dollar minimums. I was just wondering why in the world would somebody bet that much money on a card game? To the left of the blackjack tables were private rooms where celebrities or wealthy people could play without being hassled. Who knows how much money changed hands there? There were no clocks in the casino and I could easily see why the city got its nickname, the city that never sleeps. It was also easy to see who the high rollers were. They usually had a hotel employee with them, they were dressed very nicely and most of them had a beautiful, much younger woman beside them.

The tables where no one was playing still had dealers at them, standing with both hands on the table, ready for action. Beautiful cocktail waitresses were everywhere with their breasts spilling out of their tiny little dresses. They provided free drinks to anyone that was gambling, making a nice living on tips.

As we exited the casino, we made our way to the hotel area. We passed a security guard who asked to see our room key, no doubt in an attempt to keep the call girls and malcontents always. We found the elevator and made our way to the twenty fifth floor where we each had our own room. The suite that I was given was huge, although I still had the feeling that hotel surveillance cameras were on me. The bathroom had a garden tub and a separate glass shower. The sleeping area had a king sized bed with tons of pillows on it, then you could step down to a living area with a couch, two chairs and a meeting area. I settled in then met my friends for lunch.

We ate on the second floor of the Venetian. It was marvelous. The ceilings were painted to look like a blue sky so that no matter what time it was, it always looked like the middle of the afternoon. The second floor was also a shopping mall with shop after name brand shop for as far as you could see. A river ran through the middle of the second floor with Gondola rides that took you all around the hotel. I was convinced that you would almost always lose in Las Vegas. Someone had to pay for this luxury and it wasn't the people that lived in Las Vegas. I also got the feeling that the mafia still had a hand in Vegas. They had to, there was too much money to be made here. The only difference between the old Vegas and the new Vegas was that the Mafia got smart, they hired computer nerds and great businessmen to run the show.

We ate lunch in a fancy Italian restaurant. It was a bit too fancy for my taste. The only thing on the menu that I would eat was ravioli. My friends feasted on seafood but I am just not a seafood guy. My idea of a nice dinner is Ruth's Chris steakhouse. We were instructed to return to Jason's room after lunch to receive our instructions. Our spirits were high because the festive atmosphere of Las Vegas is contagious. We went back to Jason's room, found the television and pressed play on the DVR. John Simmons once again appeared before us.

"Hey boys. You are in my favorite weekend getaway spot in the world. I love Las Vegas so I knew from the beginning that it had to be in The Ultimate Challenge. You are going to be here for twenty four hours from the time that you checked into your rooms. Each of you will be given five thousand dollars to gamble with. Whatever you win is yours to keep. There is one thing that you have to do though. And boy do I wish that I was there to see it. You have to vote for one member of your team to sing tonight at a concert. It has to be the guy that hates to sing the most. I know who I would pick but I will let you guys decide. Have fun Mark!" John was laughing as he disappeared from the screen.

THE ULTIMATE CHALLENGE

My heart sunk as I heard those words. My so called friends were all doubled over in laughter. I was scared to death. My big mouth had caused this problem. In college I confessed one night that I would rather face a den of hungry lions than have to sing in front of a crowd. It was my worst nightmare.

"Please do not make me do this" I pleaded with my teammates.

"You are doing it, baby!" Drew said between bursts of laughter.

"Whew! This is going to be good." Eric exclaimed.

I looked at Jason hoping for support but deep inside I knew better. "It is time to take one for the team."

"If we win I will give one million dollars to anyone who takes my place."

"I wouldn't take five million" Drew answered. "Some things are priceless and this is one of them."

This challenge had definitely made their day and ruined mine.

"Well if I have to do this, I am not doing it sober. It just wouldn't happen."

"Drink all you want. Do what you have to do. We don't care. This is going to be the funniest thing that I have ever seen!" boasted Eric.

"What are you going to sing?" Jason asked while trying to hold in his laughter.

"I don't know!" I shouted.

This drew another round of laughter. They were all staring at me with goofy grins on their faces. I was not amused.

"None of you understand! I do not sing! I don't even sing in front of my wife. I do not dance. I don't do any of that crap."

"Well you are singing tonight!" Drew shouted while trying his best to churn butter like he always did when he got excited. All three of my teammates were high fiving each other and laughing their butts off, all at my expense. The fun of The Ultimate Challenge was back, at least for everyone but me."

"Drew, why don't you go up there and sing your stupid version of The Devil Went Down to Georgia like you did in front of that crowd in college?"

"No chance my friend. It is not going to happen" he replied with certainty in his voice.

My singing career began and ended in church choir when I was a kid. I even hated it then, but my mom made me go. Back then, I just mouthed the words as the other kids sang. If I only had that luxury tonight. I have played ball in front of some large crowds but that was something that I was pretty good at. I only sang in the shower or in the car when I was alone. I did sing little songs that I made up to Thomas when we were alone but that was it. The thought of quitting the race actually entered my mind. That is how much that I hate to sing. I used to duck out of karaoke night at corporate meetings. I was even too embarrassed to dance with Susan in the privacy of our own home. I loved listening to music but that was where my comfort zone ended. I have a pretty good voice, I can carry a tune, but something inside of me is just scared to death of singing in public. And now, I am going to be in front of God knows how many people singing a solo. I would rather be beaten and left for dead than sing a song in front of a crowd.

Crazy thoughts started entering my mind. I could call in a bomb scare or start a fire. Some people are afraid of heights and other are claustrophobic. Me, I have singophobia. My friends could look at my face and see that I was ruined for the day so they went down to the casino. I went back to my room to think

THE ULTIMATE CHALLENGE

things over. I was just going to have to suck it up. My first thought was that these people would never see me again but then I remembered that it would be aired on the Expedition Channel. My wife, parents, friends and everyone watching would see it. There would be jokes by late night talk show hosts. This thing would haunt me forever. After thinking for a while and staring out of the window at the Las Vegas strip, I decided to just go for it. I was going to try my best and if I was terrible, I would just laugh it off like Eric laughed off his terrible hitting exhibition. Why was I even worrying about this? Yesterday I was almost killed and today I am stressing about singing a little song. I tried singing a little in my hotel room but then shuddered at the thought of doing it in front of an audience.

My practice was interrupted by a knock on the door.

"Hello" I answered.

"Mr. Holland, I am Sam Cox. I am going to be assisting you this evening."

"Come on in" I said while staring at nothing but the ground.

"Sam, I will just tell you up front that I am really stressed about doing this."

"Listen, don't worry about it. There are thousands of people that would love to have this opportunity" he explained.

"That may be true, but I am definitely not one of them."

"You are going to be the opening act for Wayne Newton tonight. The show starts at 7:30 so we will take you over around 6:00. Do you have any idea of what you might like to sing?"

"No, not really. I have never done anything even remotely similar to this before. I like Creed. Do you think the band will know anything by them?"

"I'm sure they do. They can play anything."

Maybe I could get the band to drown out my singing. "Well Creed is pretty hard, so hopefully that would drown out the sound of my voice."

Mr. Cox laughed "You really don't want to do this, do you?"

I nodded no while hanging my head in self-pity.

"Listen, we will explain to the crowd what is going on and I will make sure that they will be kind to you."

"What kind of music does Wayne Newton play?" I asked. "I have seen his picture probably one hundred times since we landed."

"He is by far the most popular entertainer in this city. You haven't been here before have you Mark? He makes a fortune performing here a few nights a week. He is a legend in this city. Do you want to practice before the show?" he asked.

"No way! Singing once is bad enough. This whole thing is terrible. I just want to sing my song and get the hell out of here. Mr. Cox, I am not a performer. I can't sing or dance. This is going to be a joke, and the joke is on me."

Chapter 22

I had three hours to waste and I was tired of worrying, so I went down to the casino to blow some money. Gambling is a lot more fun when you are playing with someone else's money. I decided to try my hand at blackjack. Drew loved gambling and he had given me a few pointers on the flight to Vegas. He said always assume that the dealer has a face card down and the dealer has to stay if he has seventeen or higher. It sounded easy enough. I sat down at the least expensive table, $10 minimum, and placed my bet. I did pretty well, I was up $30 after half an hour and then they changed the dealer on me. The terminator came in and I lost seven hands in a row. I quickly decided that the game wasn't fun anymore and went to look for my friends. Every direction that I turned, there seemed to be someone in a suit standing around. I would imagine that there was not much theft in Las Vegas. The Mafia isn't visible here but I am pretty sure that if you try to cheat the casino, you could end up six feet underground somewhere in the Nevada desert.

I found my friends at a craps table.

"Hey, there is our little song bird" Eric said.

"Hey look, it's Wayne Newton, Jr.!" Drew added.

I looked at Jason "Go ahead. It is your turn."

He didn't have anything to say. It was then that I decided to make my final plea with my friends.

"Look guys. I would really like for one of you to take my place tonight."

No one responded or even glanced at me.

I continued "Who is the person that hit the homerun? Who is the one that saved all of your butts and shot Henley? It's time for one of you to step up to the plate!"

"You're desperate aren't you?" Jason asked.

"Yes I am. Are you going to do it for me?"

"No way. I was just making an observation."

"You are singing the song! End of story" Eric added.

"Drew, what about you?"

"No chance" he replied without even looking up from the table.

I needed some fresh air so I decided to take a stroll. I left my friends and The Venetian, disgusted with the world. I took a left out of the hotel with no particular destination in mind. As I walked away, I passed a group of young Asian men that were handing out pamphlets. They forced one of the flyers into my hands so I accepted it and walked away. They handed me baseball cards. But they were no ordinary cards. They were cards with women on them. And they left nothing to the imagination. It made for a good laugh. And I needed a good laugh.

THE ULTIMATE CHALLENGE

It was a nice afternoon. It was sixty five degrees and sunny which was very unusual for the usually very hot desert around Las Vegas. I was in one of the vacation capitols of the world with money to burn, but I was miserable. I made a circle back to the Venetian and ordered a Dickel Drop. It was my favorite drink because it was made of George Dickel whiskey and Sundrop. The George Dickel distillery was located in my small hometown in Tennessee and Sundrop had a bottling company there also. It was also the best tasting drink that I had ever had. And I needed to take the edge off. It was the first of several drinks. I needed some liquid courage and I needed it fast.

My friends came up to my room to check in with me around 4:30.

"How did you guys do at the tables?" I asked.

"Jason is up a little but I am down $400" Drew answered.

"Do you know what song that you are going to sing?" Eric asked while trying to suppress a grin.

"Well, that's the problem. I only know all of the words to one song."

"Which one?" Drew asked.

"I can't say. You will all laugh."

"We won't laugh. Come on. Tell us. What is it?" Jason questioned.

I stared down at the ground as I mumbled "Somewhere over the Rainbow, from the Wizard of Oz."

"Do what?" Eric asked as if he didn't hear me clearly.

"Somewhere over the Rainbow!" I said louder with irritation in my voice.

Jason quickly excused himself into my bathroom to relieve his hysteria in private.

Drew stared at me with a surprised half grin on his face. "You are kidding, right?"

"No I am not kidding. That is the only song that I know all of the words to."

Eric covered his face with his hands and shook his head in disbelief. He tried successfully for one minute, then could no longer hold his laughter in. He broke out into laughter while simultaneously waving his hands in front of his face saying that he didn't mean to. Drew laughed also but not as hard because he could not believe what he had just heard. Jason reentered the room laughing hysterically and not trying to hide it.

Eric mustered the strength to say "Holland, you can't sing Over the damn Rainbow. There will be people there. They will laugh you off the stage."

"It is either that or a Christmas song and it is not Christmas!" I angrily replied.

"Man, I am sorry, but this is going to be the funniest thing that I have ever seen" Drew said while finally allowing himself to laugh uncontrollably.

My teammates were fully recovered from the tragedies that we had faced. I was going to have some fun with them to. I couldn't believe that they fell for it. I was not going to be singing Somewhere Over the Rainbow anywhere at any time. I was going to be just fine. Maybe even do a pretty good job. And they didn't know it but I had a few surprises for them.

THE ULTIMATE CHALLENGE

Sam Cox knocked on my door at 5:45 and we started our journey to the Tropicana Hotel.

Mark, you don't seem as nervous as when we first spoke.

"It is the miracle of George Dickel" I replied.

I was still pretty nervous but he didn't need to know it. We walked for what seemed like an hour just to get out of the Venetian and then to the hotel where I would be singing. There was someone to pick out what I wore, someone to fix my hair (which I refused) and someone to put make-up on my face (which I adamantly refused). I didn't care if I looked like a walking corpse on stage, I was not going to wear make-up. My friends already had enough ammunition. Me wearing make-up was the last thing that they needed. I told the band that we would be singing Sweet Caroline by Neil Diamond. It finally popped into my mind that the crowd would sing along with me and everyone knew that song. It was universally known and loved and everyone sang to it whenever it was played.

By 7:00, everyone was finished with me and I sat alone in my dressing room. My palms were sweating and I couldn't concentrate on any one thing to take my mind off of the song that I had to sing. I made sure that my teammates would be seated in the front row, then returned to my room, pacing nervously from one side of the room to another. I had only been this nervous once in my life, the fifteen minutes before my wedding. I had my friends and brother to chat nervously with then, but now I had no one. I looked at myself in the mirror and laughed. How in the world did I even get here? My whiskey buzz was gone and so were my nerves.

At 7:15, the worst possible scenario occurred. My two Italian Beef sandwiches from last night were knocking at my back door. Thank goodness there was a bathroom in my dressing room. I had to go and pray that I would be finished in time. I got really lucky and was washing my hands when Sam Cox poked his head in and said "Ten minutes Mr. Holland."

"Was I really going to do this?" I hoped that Susan would be watching because she was going to absolutely die. She would laugh so hard and also feel sympathy for me at the same time. The song would last for four minutes. It was such a short amount of time in the grand scheme of things. I had ruined an entire day of my life worrying about four lousy minutes.

I was dressed like a cheese ball. I had allowed the wardrobe guys to dress me in exchange for not touching my head in any way. I was wearing black pants, a t-shirt and a black coat. I guess they were trying to find my inner Johnny Cash.

With two minutes left until show time, Sam came to escort me to the stage. Assistants were everywhere, each worrying about a minor last minute detail. I felt like I was making the walk down the Green Mile to my execution. I would rather fight Mike Tyson than do what I was about to do. But it was too late. Just try your best and whatever happens, happens.

I stood with the band, behind the curtain, waiting for the introduction. I could hear noise from the crowd but I had no idea what the auditorium looked like or how many people would be watching me. I stood in the semidarkness of the stage, with only a microphone in my hand, not even sure how far I should hold it away from my mouth. I was about to give myself a pep talk when the crowd erupted in applause for the announcer.

"Ladies and gentlemen, welcome to the beautiful Tropicana hotel and casino and welcome to Las Vegas. You are going to see a great show tonight. The famous Wayne Newton is here. But first, we have a special treat. The hottest show on television, The Ultimate Challenge, is filming here tonight. It is our pleasure to announce tonight that Mark Holland, one of the competitors on the show will be performing for us. This is Mark's first time to sing in front

THE ULTIMATE CHALLENGE

of a live audience so let's give him a big welcome and sing along to "Sweet Caroline."

This was it. The big moment had finally arrived. As the curtain slowly lifted, so did my anxiety level. The crowd was greeting me with warm applause but my hands were as cold as ice. I was petrified. I glanced back at the drummer and he gave me an encouraging nod. I had always heard that to not be nervous you need to picture the audience in their underwear but the lights were so bright that I couldn't see past the first two rows.

The applause slowly died and the band began the introduction to the song. I stood in front of a crowd of two thousand and I was as stiff as a board. I wasn't swaying to the music, I wasn't tapping my foot, nothing. It was at that time that I wished that I would have rehearsed the song at least once. But that was completely my fault. The main problem was that the band was already playing and I had no idea when to start singing. The band finished the intro and then started playing it again as the crowd squirmed awkwardly in their chairs. I could sense that everyone watching was pulling for me, they didn't want to see a train wreck. So I forgot about the audience, stared into the bright lights and started singing just like I was in the shower. The first five words were heard only by me until I received the courage to pull the microphone closer to my mouth. The first few lines of the song were awkward but when the crowd joined in, it really wasn't that bad. They could sense my discomfort and they just sang the song with me. Not just the chorus that everyone sings, but they sang the entire song. Thank God for Neil Diamond and the song that everyone knows. After the first verse, I was so much more comfortable and would even go as far too say that I enjoyed it. When it was over, everyone applauded and we all had a good time. My friends were standing up and leading the ovations which made me feel bad about the surprise that I had planned for them.

The old saying that what doesn't kill you makes you stronger certainly applied here. The announcer walked toward me and I handed him the microphone.

I waved to the crowd and then walked off of the stage. I remained on the side of the stage so that I could watch what was about to unfold. I was really hoping that all of our team's wives were watching. I did have a tinge of regret but they deserved it.

The announcer addressed the crowd "That was Mark Holland, ladies and gentlemen. Great job Mark. Wayne Newton will be out in just a moment but before he comes out we have another special surprise this evening."

The spotlight was on the announcer in the center of the stage as he continued "Everyone knows that in Las Vegas we love everybody. We embrace everyone and the decisions that they make. Tonight we want to recognize a very special couple. The two love birds met over a decade ago in college. They have been inseparable ever since. So to celebrate their decade long commitment to each other we are going to recognize them here tonight. They are sitting together here on the front row. Please give a special Tropicana Hotel and Casino welcome to Eric Jones and Drew Norman."

The spotlight shined on Eric and Drew as their faces turned a crimson shade of red. They stayed seated as the crowd clapped and searched for the happy couple. The announcer was a bit annoyed that they wouldn't stand up so he walked off of the stage and stood next to them and said "You are not going to get off that easy guys. Stand up and wave so that everyone can see you."

The crowd around Drew and Eric pressured them to stand up and they did. Eric was mortified but Drew always went with the moment so he grabbed Eric's hand and lifted it in the air. The announcer made the entire prank when he ended by saying "Let's hear it for love in Las Vegas."

Drew and Eric were both grinning by then. They knew that I had gotten them back and now they had to stand and take it. Not only was that for making me sing but it was also for showing my before picture with my shirt off earlier in the month. They thought that I had forgotten about that one. I peered over

THE ULTIMATE CHALLENGE

at Jason who was sitting next to them. He was about to puke from laughing so hard. His face was as red as their faces were and he could barely breathe. If he only knew what was about to happen.

It was then that I got an uneasy feeling in my stomach and kind of wished that I had not pulled this prank. The announcer was still standing next to my friends in the front row. He said "Ladies and gentlemen, we have one more surprise this evening."

Jason's unbridled laughter immediately ceased and he turned around in his seat with his eyes staring directly at his shoes.

The announcer continued. "In honor of Eric and Drew's ten year anniversary, their good friend Jason Mulkey is going to sing their song for us. Here to perform "Somewhere over the Rainbow" from the Wizard of Oz, is Mr. Jason Mulkey.

The crowd applauded as the announcer grabbed Jason's arm and led him onstage. He handed Jason the microphone and turned him toward the crowd. Jason, unknowingly, lifted the microphone up to his mouth and uttered "Oh Dear Lord."

The crowd roared with laughter as the band began to play the song. I glanced at Eric and Drew and they were literally rolling in the aisle with laughter. I was torn. On one hand, it was hilarious and he had no problem laughing at me earlier. But on the other hand, we are talking about Jason here. He was one of the quietest and mild mannered guys that I had ever met. My friends, the late John Simmons included, thought that it would be funny to make me sing. But to make Jason sing in front of hundreds of people was just cruel. It was too late now so I decided to watch.

The poor guy couldn't sing at all. His voice cracked as he awkwardly began to sing "Somewhere over the rainbow, way up high." His voice was an octave too low and he was way off tune. His face wasn't red anymore, it was a very pale white. He slowly continued "There's a land that I've heard of." Jason was in trouble and it was my fault so I knew that I had to do something. I was afraid that if I didn't, he would pass out. So I walked back onto the stage and started moving both hands for the crowd to join in the singing and thank God they did. The entire audience finished serenading Drew and Eric and the spotlight flashed back on them. It surprised both of them so they uncomfortably waved to the audience once again when the song ended. As we walked off of the stage Jason said "I am going to kill you!"

My friends had come to the Tropicana hotel ready to roast me and they left with their tails between their legs. We left before the Wayne Newton show. It would have been nice to see him, but I was too excited to sit still. My friends weren't in the mood to talk about my performance though, they just wanted sympathy for what I had put them through.

"Mark do you realize that we are going to be in every tabloid in the country" Drew said very seriously in an attempt to make me feel guilty.

"That was the idea. You show my gut on national television and make me sing in front of a crowd, then I get you back. That, my friend, is how it works."

Jason jumped in "Well there was that time in college when you two were rooming together and you got into sleeping naked. We wondered about you then. What was that all about?"

"Give me a break" Eric answered.

"Hey, what you two do under the covers is none of our business" I snidely remarked.

Drew looked at Eric "We will never win this. Just drop it."

THE ULTIMATE CHALLENGE

We made a slow walk back to the hotel, admiring the lights of the strip as we walked. The lights of Las Vegas were unbelievable. I cannot imagine their electric bill. We then made our way back to the casino for some serious gambling. I was on a natural high. To conquer a true fear felt really good. The problems of the past few days were in our rear view mirror and we were having fun again.

It was Saturday night and the Venetian casino was packed. Everyone that was there looked important. We saw a few celebrities. Eddie George was there shooting craps with Jerome Bettis. Then we saw Andrew Dice Clay and he was strutting around doing whatever Andrew Dice Clay does. He was much bigger than I would have imagined and he had a little assistant running around and attending to his every need. We were actually recognized by several people who took a few pictures with us and we even signed a few autographs. I have no idea why they wanted an autograph but I signed it very sloppily and acted as though I had done it a million times. Eric was really enjoying our fifteen minutes of fame. He was working the crowd and flirting with all of the cute women. I received more enjoyment out of watching him than I did from receiving any attention from others.

The blackjack minimums were up to fifteen dollars so we found an empty table and sat down to try our luck. Over the course of an hour, we lost two thousand dollars between us and decided that we didn't want to fund a new wing of the hotel, so we went to try our luck at the Sports Book. Eric went his own way, hoping that more women would recognize him. Jason, Drew and I studied the betting lines and decided to try our luck.

The sports book at the Venetian is a sports fan's dream. There are about twenty giant television screens all turned on to a different game being shown. The chairs are like movie seats. They are extremely comfortable and offer plenty of leg room. The lighting was dim and there was a bar behind us. The whiskey that I had consumed throughout the afternoon made the thought of another drink unimaginable so I stuck with bottled water. I put five hundred dollars on the Arizona Cardinals to win the Super Bowl. They were the only half way decent team with long shot odds and it wasn't my money anyway so I took a chance. The Cardinals had one hundred to one odds to win the Super Bowl so if the impossible happened and they won, I would pocket fifty thousand dollars. I leaned back in my chair and watched twenty Major League baseball games at once. For me, it was much more enjoyable than a casino.

What a difference this was from the Appalachian Trail. After about an hour Eric checked in with us and said that he had spotted the other team. One of the rednecks had hit a homerun out of Wrigley Field and now they were once again hot on our trail. Eric no longer had his game face on and he was taking full advantage of the complimentary drinks and he slurred his words as he talked.

"Hey Mark, the place is awesome!" he slurred.

"Yeah, it is pretty nice"

"Man that was pretty funny what you did to us tonight."

"You deserved it. Hey, you might want to lay off of the drinks. There is no telling what we have to do tomorrow."

"Don't worry about me man. I'm just getting a little buzz going" he explained as his breath practically knocked me over.

He then continued "Holland man, there are women everywhere. I have already had one to ask me to go up to the room."

"You are a married man Eric."

"You need to lighten up. This is Las Vegas. Have a little fun."

"And you need to sober up bud."

THE ULTIMATE CHALLENGE

Eric was bored with me so he left to rejoin the action. Drew and Jason were entranced into the bets that they had made on the games that they were watching.

I turned to Jason "Eric is blitzed."

"I could tell."

"I hope he doesn't do something that he regrets later."

"He is a big boy" Jason replied without taking his eyes off of the game that he was watching.

I was completely exhausted so I excused myself and went to my room. It was after midnight and the casino was just warming up. I was totally worn out from a day full of worrying but the night could not have gone better and I slept like a baby.

Chapter 23

I was woken up by a knock on the door at four in the morning. I was not happy because I was enjoying my best night's sleep in a week. I answered the door and a drunken Eric was waiting for me.

"What?" I asked in a tone that showed him that I was clearly agitated.

"You weren't asleep were you?"

"It is four in the morning. Of course I was asleep. This isn't college anymore."

"Well excuse me! I am sorry that I needed somebody to talk to."

"Come on in" I reluctantly replied.

"No, I don't want to mess up your beauty sleep."

"Get in here. I am not going to argue with you."

Eric entered the room and immediately raided the snack bar.

"So what is your problem?" I asked while getting back under the covers of my bed.

"Mark, you cannot tell this to a sole" Eric demanded.

I remembered that cameras were televising our every move so I instructed my drunken teammate to go with me to the bathroom and told him to spill it fast.

"I took a girl to my room tonight" he confessed. "She was a beautiful blond and she was begging me to sleep with her."

"Go on" I said and woke up quickly with the crazy news.

"Well, we went to my room and started kissing." He then paused and stared at the ground. "Here comes the bad part" he said in embarrassment.

"What happened" I asked trying to hurry his story along.

"Things were getting a little hot and heavy."

"Okay."

Eric was sitting on the toilet and had his hands covering his face.

"Eric, I'm not understanding you here."

"She was a prostitute."

"What?"

"She was a prostitute. She wanted me to pay."

"Whoa. Wait a second. Let me get this straight. So you thought it was a normal girl. But it was really a prostitute and she didn't tell you first?"

THE ULTIMATE CHALLENGE

"She looked normal."

That took Eric over the top. He dropped to the ground, lifted the seat on the toilet and hurled, luckily hitting his intended target.

I really didn't know what to say. And then reality hit.

"How long ago did you go up to the room?"

"It just happened. Maybe twenty minutes ago" he said between heaves.

"Okay" I said.

I immediately called Ron Craig on the cell phone and woke him from a dead sleep. I explained the situation and while I waited he called the Expedition Channel and had them remove all of the evidence. Thank God for a one hour tape delay. Even with that, we only had ten minutes to spare but luckily we saved Eric's butt. I thanked Ron and then apologized profusely for waking him.

Eric had finished puking by the time that I got off the phone. He had gone to my bed and dozed off when I made the phone call, unaware that his infidelity had been videotaped. I woke him up.

"Hey! Wake up! I just saved your drunk butt!"

"What are you talking about?" he groggily asked.

"What I mean is that your room was being videotaped. You are just too drunk to remember that!"

"Oh no. I am dead. I am so stupid."

"Hang on liquor boy. I said that I saved your butt. None of that stuff is going to air."

"Are you serious? Oh thank you. Thank you so much. I owe you big. What can I do? Just ask."

"You can get out of my room and let me sleep."

"Okay man" he answered as he stumbled over to me and gave me a hug. "I love you man" he proclaimed.

"You have done enough of that already tonight. Just let me sleep."

"Please don't tell anybody that."

"Eric, you had way too much to drink tonight. But listen to me for a second. Love your wife. Treat her like a queen. You will get out of it what you put into it."

"Thanks Mark."

"Now go to bed. We have seven hours until we are out of here. Go sleep it off."

Eric left and I finished my night's sleep.

I met Jason and Drew for a breakfast buffet the next morning. I had big plans for the buffet because we had no idea when we would eat another decent meal. Eric stayed in bed, trying his best to sleep off his hangover.

"Did you guys win last night?" I asked.

THE ULTIMATE CHALLENGE

"Actually, we both won big. The Braves, Yankees and Rangers all won. We both cleared three grand."

"Where is the little guy?" Jason asked.

"I think that he is going to sleep all that he can. The last time that I saw him he was plastered."

I kept my promise to Eric and did not mention his eventful night. I didn't lie to my friends, I just chose my words carefully.

Chapter 24

We woke Eric up at noon, thirty minutes before it was time to leave. He didn't want to get out of bed and it was easy to see that his head was pounding. We gave him an aspirin, made him take a shower and promised him that things would get better.

Once again we crowded into the small back room of the RV to receive the next destination that John Simmons had planned for us. John appeared on the screen with his usual grin and said "Well guys, I hope that you are not too hung over because you have quite a drive today. You are going to the city where I made the big bucks, San Francisco. You won't have great accommodations or beautiful girls serving you drinks. You are going to the rock. The guards will give you instructions. I hope that you all enjoyed Las Vegas because tonight you are going to be roughing it. Oh, and one more thing. The one hundred million dollars that you all will share if you win, that is after taxes!" John disappeared as we rejoiced.

"What is the rock?" Eric asked the group.

"It is Alcatraz" Drew answered.

"You mean the prison?" Eric questioned.

"No the resort" Jason sarcastically replied.

"You mean that we have to sleep in a jail with guards?" Eric asked.

"Not real guards. Alcatraz has been closed for years, dumb ass" Drew replied.

"Well excuse me mister jail expert. Man, I am a little bit claustrophobic. Guys, I still don't feel good, do you mind if I sleep?" Eric continued.

"You can do anything you want if you will just shut up. You are getting on my nerves you little Smurf."

"Shut up Holland" Eric added as he disappeared under the covers.

"Jason drove and I navigated as Drew played solitaire on the kitchen table. "Well, what did you think of Las Vegas?" I asked Jason.

"I loved it man. I want to come back here and vacation someday" he answered as we were leaving the city limits. Cars honked and people waved as we were once again trying to distance ourselves between ourselves and the rednecks.

"What did you like about it?" Jason asked.

"The whole singing thing kind of ruined my stay but I would come back here someday. You should have seen your face when you found out that you had to sing also" I laughed while picturing Jason's face at that moment.

"That was the worst possible thing that you ever could have done to me" Jason replied.

"Join the club. I don't remember you having much pity for me either. The worst thing that I could have done was make you sing the song all by yourself. I am just glad that you are taking it so well."

THE ULTIMATE CHALLENGE

Jason let out a small laugh "It was mean. Mean as hell. But we had it coming."

"I have always wanted to go to Alcatraz" I said, changing the subject.

"Yeah, me too" Jason answered. "But I would rather just tour it, not sleep there."

"Yeah, it may be a little eerie."

"And uncomfortable. How far behind us do you think the rednecks are?" Jason asked.

"Maybe a few hours. Tops. We have to keep pushing it. No more alcohol. Eric couldn't handle it. He can do that after the race. It is time to perform now."

"We will push it until we get to the finish line" Jason replied. "Have you thought much about what you want to do if we win?"

"Yeah, do you want to hear about it?"

"We have got nothing but time" he answered.

"Well, my plans have changed a little bit since he told us that the money is after taxes. Do you realize that the amount of money that the winner gets just doubled?"

"Yes I do. I can't even imagine one million much less twenty five."

"The first thing that I would do is put half of it in safe investments. It will always be there so I can change my family tree for generations. Then I will make a big donation to cancer research in honor of John. And I saw this documentary on ESPN where these guys made a pact to run across the Sahara desert to raise money for charity. It was crazy. They found people in the middle of the desert that would walk for two days to get water and leave their seven year old kid alone in sand storms until they got back."

"That is crazy!" Jason said.

"Here is the crazy part. There is actually good fresh drinking water under the desert. It's just hundreds of feet under it. So these guys that ran started a charity to dig wells to get to that water. So I will make a donation to them. I just don't understand why someone hasn't done it already."

"That sounds like a pretty good charity to me. I am going to watch it when we get home. I will contribute too."

"That will leave me about ten million bucks. I will buy a nice house, an Audi sports car, stuff like that. And I have this plan that I have thought about for years. It sounds a little crazy but I think it might work."

"What is it?"

"You know that my career was selling baseball stuff. So I have gotten to meet all of these different coaches. And the one thing that always baffled me was that every coach had a different story about a kid with tons of talent that for whatever reason didn't make it. I saw it for myself. I actually saw a kid that could throw a baseball one hundred three miles an hour. And his curveball was his best pitch. It was nasty. It was the best curve ball that I have ever seen. And his change-up was terrific. He had three pitches that scouts would consider as Major League ready. He was that good."

"That sounds like that old Sid Finch story that Sports Illustrated made up for April fool's day" Jason said as he looked at me skeptically.

"I swear that I saw it with my own two eyes. The only problem was that he had absolutely no control. He would start a game and look like Cy Young for

THE ULTIMATE CHALLENGE

two innings. Then he would come out and walk three batters, throw four or five wild pitches, hit a couple of guys in the head and then he was done. It was so sad. And he was a good kid. He got drafted but didn't get past single A. Every problem that he had was in his head."

"That is tragic. So what is your point?"

"My point is that I would move back to Tullahoma, TN where we both grew up. It is a baseball haven that most people don't know about. I would build a facility that is state of the art. I would then use my contacts in college and the big leagues to find out who those players are that had all of the talent in the world, but just couldn't make it work. Then, I would put together a group of coaches, sports psychiatrists and trainers to work with those athletes to work through their issues and get them on the right path."

"That sounds great and all but don't you think that the teams that drafted these guys have already tried that? I mean who would spend a bunch of money on a guy and then just watch him melt down?"

"I'm with you there. But here is the key. Most of those guys that melt down are young, like in their mid-twenties or even younger. A couple of years after they have given up, they are so much more mature. And with the right therapy and technique maybe they could turn into the player that everyone thought they would be."

"It is a great idea but I am a little skeptical about how effective it would be and how you would fund it long term."

"That is the greatest part. You start out with one major league team. If you sell them on the idea and show them that you will invest, then it is chump change for them to throw a couple of million at it. Then you get the player involved and have an agreement that if they make it to the big leagues, a small portion of their salary every year goes to it. They never would have made it without our help. So it is a no brainer. It is one of those things that I have always thought about but never had the time or money to implement."

"You really have thought this through. But when you get a guy ready, where does he play to see if it all blows up when he gets into a game?

"I am not sure. Maybe with the clubs rookie team. And then work from there. The key is in the mental aspect of each person's game. I have seen hitters that could hit any fastball that you throw at them but they can't touch off speed pitches. That is where the team of coaches, trainers and mental professionals come together and put together a game plan. If a plan is put together that allows each player to reset their mind when the wheels are about to fall off, then I think we have something."

"How in the world would you put all of these professionals together?"

"I don't know yet but if we win this race, there will be plenty of time to put it together. It is one of those things that I wouldn't really even want to make money on. Eventually, I would want it to sustain itself and if we start pumping out guys that turn out to be great ballplayers, we have got it made."

Jason mulled over the idea for a moment. "The way that I look at it is that the key to this whole thing working is finding the right players with the right mindset that really want to make it. The problem that you have is that you will be finding players that have already hung up the cleats. They have already quit."

"But they quit only because they didn't see a solution to their problem. Right? Think about it for a second. If you could throw a baseball one hundred miles an hour which only a few people can do in the major leagues, you have a nasty curve ball and a really good change-up, when you got out of the game for a couple of years don't you think that you would want another shot?"

THE ULTIMATE CHALLENGE

"Let me play the devil's advocate for a minute" Jason said. "Let's say that you can do all of those things but you are embarrassed repeatedly because you can't get a handle on it, then why would you want to come back? They didn't leave the game because they wanted to. People gave up on them."

"That is where your point about finding the right people comes in. And that is where Tullahoma, TN comes in. It is in the middle of nowhere. You have to start out with a no pressure environment for these athletes. Get their mind right, get there technique right and then somehow increase that pressure while maintaining the same mind and same techniques."

"Your plan seems good and everything but the problem that I see is getting the right team of professionals together to make the thing work. You see players trying to come back all of the time and it almost never works."

"As far as the coaches and mental health people goes, I think that you need to search for people that have wondered the same thing that I have. I would want to find a team of coaches and sports psychologists that have asked themselves the same exact questions and always thought that they could really help certain people. They would have to have a crazy passion for rehabilitation as I do. As far as the players go, most comebacks come from people that were physically hurt. I wouldn't want to try to physically fix them, but find guys that could be mentally fixed."

"If you put this thing together and we win this race, then I would love to be in on it to. How cool would it be to turn on the television and see a guy dominate in the Major Leagues that you had a hand in fixing."

"You have it now. That is the whole agenda that I have. It is not about the money but it is about seeing people with extraordinary talent reach their dreams."

"And getting great seats whenever you want to see them play" Jason replied.

"Oh yeah. Totally."

We had driven for two hours and it had seemed like ten minutes. We could have talked about our dream for days, but we didn't dare, we were too afraid of jinxing ourselves. I couldn't stop my mind from working though and my dream would not leave my head. I propped my feet up on the dashboard and stared silently into the Nevada desert without really seeing a thing. My mind was already putting it all together.

Chapter 25

My dream came to a grinding halt as the engine in our 2013 Ford Tracker sputtered then died. Jason shifted the gear into neutral and we glided to the side of the interstate. Drew felt us slowing and woke up from his nap in a reclining chair that was behind us.

"What happened?" he asked.

"I don't know" Jason replied. "It just died."

"We have got to fix it quick" I said. "Drew, go take a look."

Drew was our only hope because he was the only person on our team with any knowledge of engine problems. The rest of us exited our vehicle and stared at the engine as Drew examined it, as if that would help. As Drew examined under the hood, I called Ron Craig.

"Ron, we have a problem. The RV died on us."

"Do you know what is wrong?" he asked.

"Drew is looking at it, but it doesn't look good."

"I will call the guys at the Expedition Channel to pinpoint your location then get a van out to you as quick as possible. That is the best that I can do."

"So you mean that the other team can close the gap on us because a vehicle that you provided is broken?" I asked hoping for some type of relief.

"It is part of the game Mark. You know that. Hold on and I will give you an ETA on the van."

I was on hold for five minutes and could sense the rednecks getting closer with every passing second. In the meantime, Drew diagnosed the problem and it was not fixable, the transmission was shot.

Ron finally returned "Mark, you guys are in the middle of nowhere."

"You don't have to tell me that" I sarcastically answered.

"I have got a van on the way, but it is going to be an hour and a half and that is with a police escort."

"That is unacceptable Ron" I sternly remarked.

"It has to be acceptable. It is the only choice."

"After all that we have been through, to have the lead is a miracle in itself, and now this. This is just a bunch of crap!"

"I am so sorry Mark" Ron said in his most sympathetic voice.

I turned around and faced my dejected teammates. "It is going to be an hour and a half." I received no response. All heads were down as the wind was taken completely out of our sails. We went from the penthouse to the outhouse in a matter of minutes. We began the waiting game and raided the snack bar in

THE ULTIMATE CHALLENGE

our broken RV. It was 3:30 in the afternoon, the sun was hot and so were our tempers.

Eric woke up in a bad mood and blamed it on everyone else. "I can't even sleep for a couple of hours without something going wrong" he said.

"Oh yeah, it was my fault that the transmission went out" Jason sarcastically shot back.

"What would you have done differently?" I asked Eric.

"I know how to drive without ruining a transmission!"

In a failed attempt to loosen things up Drew said "Eric, you can barely see over the steering wheel, you don't even pass the height requirements to drive this thing."

"Ha. Ha." Eric angrily answered.

"Lay off of him" I screamed at Drew. "He brought his booster seat."

This drew a healthy round of laughter from Jason and Drew but Eric did not find it amusing.

"What are you laughing at, you timid wimp?" Eric angrily asked Jason.

"I am laughing at you, you stupid midget!" Jason said as he laughed.

"Jason, that wasn't very nice at all" Drew said. "They are called little people now."

Everyone was laughing at Eric because his attitude deserved it and he needed to be knocked down a bit. He was at his wits end.

"I have had enough of the short shit!" Eric screamed at the top of his lungs. "I don't make fun of you, so don't make fun of me! I am serious. Enough!" Veins were bulging out of Eric's forehead as he spoke. His face exuded the anger that he felt. Never mind the fact that he had totally made fun of each one of us as often as he could.

Silence fell over the group until Drew spoke up to make amends. "Eric, I am sorry. We are all sorry. I feel really small right now. We have really short changed you" he added as Jason and I looked away to laugh.

Eric was out of patience so he flung open the door and stormed out of the RV. We were then reduced to staring at our watches as time slowed to a crawl. An hour passed, then we reached the hour and a half mark with no sign of a van. Two hours after we had made the call to Ron Craig, we finally heard a vehicle approaching on the desolate highway. Thank God. They had finally arrived. We all jumped from our seats and exited the RV. We grabbed our essentials and were ready for a quick transition to the van.

As the vehicle approached, we could see that it wasn't a van at all. It was the rednecks. Team Nike slowed as they approached us, but not to help. They were clapping and laughing wildly as they approached us at five miles an hour. Jason, our most peaceful team member, stared at them expressionless, lifted his right hand and raised his middle finger. This angered the rednecks and they slammed on their breaks while screaming at us through their rolled up windows. After a moment they regained their senses, sped off and left us in their dust.

Chapter 26

The Ultimate Challenge had just undergone its fifth lead change which was great for television ratings but terrible for our team. We tried to maintain an even keel but it was impossible with the stakes being as high as they were. For two days we had been hunted by the other team, now we were the hunters. The lead change affected our entire mentality. When our RV broke down, we were angry. Now that we were behind, we were desperate. The jokes stopped and we all focused our attention on a way to get out of this mess. We were at the mercy of others. After two more angry phone calls to Ron Craig, our van finally arrived. Their excuse was that they had to install a governor to keep our speed at seventy miles an hour, then they noticed that the van had one low tire so they had to replace it. The rednecks lead was over an hour by the time that we started again.

The rest of our drive was quiet as our stomachs were turning from the continual bad luck that we seemed to encounter. We assured each other that a one hour lead was nothing. The only thing that we knew for sure was that the race ended at Stone Mountain, Georgia and we were about as far away from Georgia as we could get. There was plenty of time to overtake the other team and we were still sure that in the end Team Reebok would prevail.

We arrived in San Francisco under the cover of darkness but it was still easy to see that the city was very unique and beautiful. The combination of surrounding mountains and the ocean made for a spectacular view. We made our way down to a dock near Fisherman's Wharf where a boat was waiting for us. We were amazed at the dramatic incline of the streets. I had seen San Francisco on television many times but I had no idea how steep the streets really were. I was driving the van and even though we were in a big hurry, I slowed down to a stop twice before driving down a steep street. My friends were complaining, but the drop off was so steep that you literally could not see the street below. If seemed like you could fall off of the face of the earth if you drove forward. We finally made it down to the pier where a crowd had gathered to watch us board our boat.

As we approached the dock, we were greeted by two men that were dressed as prison guards. They greeted us as we boarded the boat and began our fifteen minute ride to Alcatraz. The weather was cold and dreary. A steady rain soaked our clothes and a biting wind added to the misery. Alcatraz was lit up all around the island and my first impression was that it looked smaller than I had imagined. I had seen "Escape from Alcatraz" probably fifty times and I was definitely intrigued by the famous prison. To our left was another famous landmark. The Golden Gate Bridge was beautifully lit and was actually much larger than I had imagined it. As we approached Alcatraz, the boat circled the island to the right before docking on the opposite side of San Francisco. The prison was showing its age but it still commanded respect as our country's most famous prison.

The guards helped us off of the boat and spoke to us as we walked. "Gentlemen, welcome to The Rock. You will remain on Alcatraz for a period of twenty four hours. You will each be confined to individual cells in different areas of the prison. You will be provided with dinner tonight and three hot meals tomorrow. Over the next twenty four hours you will not be permitted to exit your cell for any reason. If you do request to leave, your team will forfeit the race. Buckets will be provided for your waste and the island will be closed to tourists until you leave."

I was a little excited and for some reason a little freaked out at the same time. I was going to be spending the next twenty four hours in solitary confinement.

THE ULTIMATE CHALLENGE

John Simmons must have really enjoyed creating the ups and downs of every leg of this race. We always seemed to go from luxury to somewhere dreary with every new challenge. He had us going from room service to slop buckets. We made our way past the gift shop, up two flights of stairs and into the prison. Two additional men dressed as guards greeted us inside of the prison and we were escorted to our luxury rooms for the night. My cell was in the middle of the prison on the first floor. I didn't see any members of the other team on my floor so they were obviously in another area of the prison. Alcatraz was gloomy damp and cold. It amazed me that such a miserable place was located less than a mile from arguably the most luxurious city in the country. My guard left me after locking the door and telling me that my dinner would arrive shortly. John Simmons was not kidding when he said that our mentality and emotions would be challenged. I am positive that if he knew in advance what our team was going to actually go through, he would have just left this leg of the race out completely.

My cell was tiny. I had always pictured a prison cell as being a little smaller than the bedroom that I grew up in, but I was wrong. My wingspan could touch both walls when facing the front. From the front to the back of the cell could not have been longer than eight feet. I had a hard bed and a blanket, a bucket to pee and crap in and a sink that no longer worked. The walls were painted a dull light green, another feature that added to the dreary atmosphere. I thought about the men that lived and died there and how insanity must have been inevitable. There was no television, no radio, no anything. Just silence. My thoughts turned to Al Capone, the most glorified mobster in history. He went from a life of luxury to a life of misery here on the rock. Only the worst prisoners were sent to Alcatraz and it was easy to see that it was no place for rehabilitation. Alcatraz was designed to break men down.

My dinner arrived after half an hour and I ate very slowly and deliberately. I savored every bite of the warm beef stew. The only comfort that I really found was knowing that my friends were somewhere in the prison enduring the same exact thing. I had always wondered what life would be like in prison. I always imagined that I could take it. I would just read a lot and work out all of the time. I was so naïve. I could barely handle life for one day with no prisoner's there to intimidate me. Things often seem better in your mind than actual reality. I knew after two hours in Alcatraz that the life was not for me. The lights went out two hours after dinner was served, so I used the bathroom in my little bucket and laid down on the bed. The thing that I never imagined when I thought about life in prison was the magnitude of loneliness that you feel. The feeling of being trapped somewhere was also very powerful. And to think that there are people in the world that are not in prison but they are trapped in their own world, unable to escape their reality. How lucky was I. Before the race started in the luxury of my home when I turned on the television I would see so many people with radically different views and they would yell and scream at each other. Then, they would return to wherever they lived and have plenty of food and a bed to rest their head on. I wondered how often they put things into context. To be free and able to come and go as you please was a pretty good deal.

After thinking that I had solved all of the world's problems, my thoughts turned to Susan and Thomas. I wondered what they were doing, if Thomas was wondering what happened to me. That kid could always cheer me up. I thought about his beautiful smile and all of the faces that he made to get me to laugh. I thought about Susan and all of the sacrifices that she was making to raise a small child by herself during this race. Then I thought about John Simmons and the lessons that he was trying to teach us. He wanted us to live our lives to the fullest while we were here. He wanted to take us out of our comfort zones and realize that our biggest fears weren't that crazy when we conquered them. And obviously, he realized a little too late that he let good friendships go when life got in the way. He wanted to make sure that we understood that we should never let good friendships go away. And I think that the point of bringing us to Alcatraz was for us to take stock of what we already had. To appreciate how lucky we were. I think that he also enjoyed thinking up ways to torture us a little bit. He was always underrated in my book. He wasn't an honor student in college and he didn't always need the limelight. But he was smart, practical and he could always sense opportunity. That is why he made so much money. He saw the opportunity and he went for it. He did a pretty good job in constructing

THE ULTIMATE CHALLENGE

The Ultimate Challenge. The audience was definitely entertained. So far, the challenge had mirrored his life. It was a combination of working hard for a while and then having fun after working. He had given us some tough tasks, but also rewarded us with some challenges that were only dreams for most people.

My daydreaming took me away from my surroundings but it did nothing for my stiff mattress, no pillow and the fact that I was freezing. After two hours of tossing, turning and feeling sorry for myself, I finally dozed off.

I woke up from a nightmare and sat straight up in bed, petrified. I may have even screamed out loud but I was not sure. I looked at my watch because the lights were back on. It was 9:30 A.M. My dream was horrific to even think about. I didn't want to go back to sleep with the fear that my dream would pick back up where it left off. John Albert Henley was not going to haunt my dreams anymore for now. I noticed that breakfast had been left for me, so I enjoyed the then cold eggs and bacon. An hour later I was growing restless so I paced my cell from one end to the other, time after time after time. The thought of totally freaking out crossed my mind but I took control of myself and did push-ups to the point of exhaustion. It was then that I accepted the fact that I just had to wait it out for ten more hours and then I would be free again. I tried to remember the last time that I had spent an entire day in total silence and came to the conclusion that it had never happened. There were so many times that I had longed for silence. Now the silence was driving me crazy so everyone that was bored enough to be watching on television was treated to the second live concert of my singing career. I sang any song that I could think of. It went from the Eagles to Garth Brooks to the songs that I made up to sing to Thomas. Anything to make noise.

At least the prisoners in Alcatraz had neighbors and cell mates. I would have loved to have a convicted felon to chat with. After a few hours I concluded that the only way to stay sane in prison would be to engulf yourself in books to take you away to another world. Then I thought about the guys with life sentences with no hope of ever leaving. Living out a life sentence in Alcatraz might have been worse than a death sentence. As much as I hated being stuck in that cell, I think that every person should spend at least one day in prison because after it is all over you can really appreciate something that you never gave a second thought about, freedom.

The most mundane tasks became major events of my day. I must have spent twenty minutes re-lacing my shoes. I took the strings out of one shoe and then the other. I then carefully inserted the laces evenly in the top holes where the laces go. Next, I inserted one side in one hole very slowly and meticulously. Then I went to work on the other side. I did this six times on each shoe until my Reeboks were perfectly re-laced. I was so bored that the highlight of my afternoon was a zit that I found on my shoulder. The job was tough because I didn't have the benefit of a mirror. I stared at the blemish for as long as I could stand it, examining every possible angle that I could strike from. I determined the angle that would give me the greatest explosion and went in for the kill. I pinched my shoulder with all of the strength that my fingers could muster and then Boom! The zit exploded with tremendous force and it definitely would have had a mirror shot if a mirror had been available.

I then went to work on my two day old beard, plucking out any hair that my fingers could grip. The task would have been much easier with the benefit of a mirror. I was that bored. Luckily my body was spared when my lunch finally arrived at 1:30. I pleaded with the guard to find me something to read but I had no luck. I spoke continually as he slid my lunch through the bars. He ignored my questions as he was obviously under strict orders not to speak with us. I was disappointed when he left but my attention quickly turned to the lunch that was sitting in front of me. I had a ham sandwich with lettuce and mustard, plain Lays potato chips and a small pack of Oreo cookies for dessert. A Dasani bottle of water was also given to me. I was determined to stretch lunch into the late afternoon, so I ate each piece of ham separately. Then I slowly devoured the lettuce. After that, I ate the bottom bun, taking very small bites. I saved the top bun for last because it had sesame seeds on it. I picked the seeds off of the bun and ate them all before finishing the bun. The chips were next. I broke the

THE ULTIMATE CHALLENGE

large ones into pieces to prolong the feast. I saved the chips that were doubled over for next to last and the burnt ones were last. I love the burnt ones. After every morsel of my sandwich and chips were gone, I opened the Oreos. I had six cookies to enjoy. I broke the first one in half, leaving the filling perfectly on one side. I ate the bald half of the cookie first, then carefully ate the white filling next, making sure not to bite any part of the cookie at the same time. After an hour and a half, my lunch was finally gone, but my entire bottled water would be enjoyed for hours.

I carefully read every word of my potato chip, cookie and water wrappers. For the first time in my life, I eagerly read slogans, ingredients and nutritional facts. By early evening I was starting to be depressed. I had seven long hours left so I laid on my cot and took a two hour nap. The guard woke me with dinner at 6:30. I devoured my spaghetti much quicker than lunch because I could sense the end of my prison term. My depression lifted as each minute passed. I would soon be a free man.

I tried to focus my mind on the challenge. The rednecks were ahead of us by at least an hour. Our stay in Alcatraz would be an experience that I would never forget but it was also frustrating during our twenty four hours because there was no way to make up time on the redneck's lead. We needed a challenge where we had to use our legs. The RV had a restrictor plate so we couldn't close the gap by driving. I was hoping for a long bicycle ride or another hike so that we could close the gap on them.

The last hour of my prison term was the worst. I was restless and agitated. I did more pushups but the only thing that it accomplished was tiring me out. I spent the last thirty minutes leaning against the bars with my arms outside of the cell. At least they could be free.

When the guard opened the latch which opened my door, I shot out of my hellhole like a bolt of lightning. I was elated to be free and walked briskly toward the exit. When I saw my friends I hugged them all which made each of them look at me funny. We wasted no time in heading to the boat without even a glance back at the Rock. My friends were as happy as I was to be free and we chatted on our boat ride like we had not seen each other in years. We didn't care what our next challenge was, we all just wanted to be moving.

As we pulled up to the dock, a large crowd was waiting to send us off. I was taken back a bit by the noise, something that I had grown used to before our stay in Alcatraz. The crowd was a little intimidating. I had spent the past twenty four hours hoping for any kind of noise but now I just wanted to get away from it. We rushed to a waiting taxi that was going to take us to the airport. Our spirits were high as we tried to guess where we might be going next. We gave up very quickly because our deceased friend was much more creative than we were.

Chapter 27

Johns Simmons plane was waiting and we boarded quickly, not as impressed this time because we had seen it before. The only difference this time was that there were four other men on board. We greeted them awkwardly as we made our way to the television where John once again appeared.

He already had a smile on his face. "Well boys, are you stir crazy yet? If you are, don't worry because I am about to send you on the wildest ride of your lives. My jet is taking you to Memphis but you are not going to land, you guys are jumping out. That's right, you are going skydiving. It was one of the great thrills of my life. The guys that you see on the plane are going to be strapped to your back. Don't worry, they are skydiving experts. Have fun and I wouldn't eat much if I were you."

I immediately looked at Jason with an uneasy expression of shock. Whether we wanted to or not, we were about to go skydiving. I had always said that I would like to try it but in a macho I will never get around to it sort of way. Not only were we about to do it but we were already on the way. I had never really put a lot of thought into what actually happens when you skydive. You jump out of an airplane and drop as fast as the weight of your body allows you. You fall for thousands of feet and then risk your entire life on a combination of cloth and ropes working perfectly to prevent you from bouncing off of the ground. All of a sudden, this sounded like the most stupid concept that I had ever heard of. You spend your entire life trying to stay out of harm's way, then for no good reason you celebrate all of those years of being careful by betting that a parachute will open. What kind of a hobby is that?

I actually grew up with a family of skydivers but until now I never realized the daring feat that they had accomplished. My mom jumped to celebrate her fiftieth birthday. I remember it like it was yesterday. I was pitching that day for my summer league baseball team. My family usually attended every game that I was pitching in and I wondered why no one came to watch me that day. I was getting rocked on the mound and I remember stepping off of the pitching rubber to regain my composure. I took a stroll behind the pitcher's mound and looked up to the sky for some divine intervention. The local airport was about half a mile away and as I looked up to the heavens, I saw five parachutes floating down to the ground. We lost the game and I came home dejected but my entire family was there and eager to show me a video. I was shocked that I had actually been watching my mom in one of those parachutes. She had not told me beforehand because she didn't want me worrying about her while I tried to pitch. The other skydiver in my family is my little brother Keith. Keith really got into skydiving. In college, he became a member of the Duke Sky-Devils and had performed over sixty jumps. Keith was always a daredevil and begged me to try it, but I never took him up on his offer. If they could do it, then I could also. I had an uneasy feeling in my stomach and the occasional turbulence that we were experiencing didn't help matters.

One of the skydivers on the plane had to take us through a short class before we made our jump. My jumping partner's name was Mario. To my relief he told me that he had performed over one thousand jumps. He would be strapped to my back and after we jumped he would let out what was called a drag shoot to slow our free fall down a bit. He explained that it was required with a tandem jump. We would free fall for about one minute before opening the parachute. As he spoke, I nervously looked out of the small window next to my seat. We were so high that I couldn't even see the ground because of the clouds.

THE ULTIMATE CHALLENGE

Mario was about forty years old with salt and pepper hair. I was as friendly to him as I had ever been to anyone in my life because my well-being was in his hands. He explained that on the count of three we would dive out of the plane just like you dive into a swimming pool. After that, you just spread your arms apart and stick your chest out as far as you can. Doing that would put you parallel to the ground and in a good position to open your shoot. He went over how to make yourself turn right or left but I didn't really care about that. I just wanted to go down. Then he gave us instructions on what to do after the shoot opens. He showed us where the string was to open the shoot but I would let him take care of that. He explained that we would have two handles when the shoot opens. If you pull down on the right one you turn to the right, the other side turns you to the left. If you pull down on both handles, it causes you to practically stop. He gave us assurances that skydiving was perfectly safe and we nodded with cautious optimism. That was it. We were prepared to jump out of a plane.

When people are nervous, they react in very different ways. Eric and Drew both laugh a lot and talk endlessly about nothing. Jason and I were different. When we were nervous, we didn't say anything. We answered questions in short mumbles and repressed into another world.

I tried to make a deal with God about going to church more, giving more and volunteering more. Just let me land on the ground. And then I added land on the ground softly. We found out that we were going to be landing in West Memphis, Arkansas then go over the bridge into Memphis for our next challenge. That was the only thing that we heard for the next hour and a half. Drew and Eric spoke nonstop with the skydivers while Jason and I stared silently into space. We were asked several times if we were okay and we lied and said yes. I was definitely nervous. I think that the main reason was because I wasn't going to be in control. I am a little bit of a control freak. It is a pretty significant fault of mine. I don't do well when I have to depend on others to get things done. I would rather do it myself, my way. Poor Susan never got to drive when I was with her because I am a terrible passenger.

With forty-five minutes left before the jump, we began to prepare. We put on thick suits similar to what I have seen skydivers wear in the movies. Everything zipped up around your clothes. Next we put on these goofy leather helmets that made us look like World War II fighter pilots. Ten minutes before we jumped, Mario strapped himself to me in six different places. He was right behind me as we both stood there waiting for the signal. He was way up into my business but that was how it was going to have to be. I was really nervous now so I spoke to Jason who looked terribly uncomfortable with a man strapped right behind him.

"Well, I guess that position is nothing new for you" I said without drawing anything but a tiny grin for a response. As we approached the drop zone I gave myself a silent pep talk. Just walk up to the door and do it. You will be on the ground in ten minutes.

Moments before the door opened, I made myself a promise. When The Ultimate Challenge was over, win or lose, I was not going to do anything that even resembled an adventure for at least a year. In less than a week we had lived in the mountains, encountered a protective bear, witnessed a murder, shot a guy, witnessed his murder, spent time in prison and we were about to jump out of an airplane. Unless we caught Team Nike, it was all for nothing. In less than ten minutes I would be on the ground.

The door opened and it was game time. The pilot slowed down and the engine hushed to a purr. Mario and I were the first in line to jump, so I glanced at each of my friends one last time.

"Go get 'em Mark." Drew shouted.

"Holland! Get fired up!" Eric added.

I looked at Jason "Happy diving."

THE ULTIMATE CHALLENGE

Mario and I made our way to the open door. We had to walk in sync and in baby steps. I approached cautiously staring straight ahead and placed my hands on each side of the plane door that we were about to exit. We had to jump quickly so that the others would be within the drop zone. I leaned out of the open door and the wind was very loud. I was glad to have the goofy leather helmet to cover my ears. I looked down at the ground and the moment seemed surreal to me. The tiny specks below were a picture that I had seen, not real life. Mario screamed directly into my ear so that I could hear him.

"One. Two."

I clinched my fists and tightened my entire body as I convinced myself to go for it.

"Three" Mario said and we were off.

I do not remember the flip that we did as we jumped out of the plane because my eyes were closed. I immediately opened them and remembered the instructions that I had been given. I bowed my chest out as far as it would go and spread my arms open wide. The roller coaster feeling of dropping only lasted for a brief second. We weren't falling, we were flying! I was not scared at all, it was the most awesome feeling in the world. I felt like Superman soaring through the air. The specks on the ground were still specks and I felt invincible. I did make the mistake of opening my mouth and my lips flapped around helplessly. I then forced my mouth to close and once again continued enjoying my ability to fly. The wind was deafening as we cut through it at incredible speed. I was traveling faster than I had ever deemed possible, a speed so great that it would have put any race car to shame. Now, I finally understood why people loved this sport. It was a natural high that was more addictive than any drug could ever be. It was a feeling of power like nothing else that I had ever felt. It was quite simply the definition of euphoria. It was a feeling that no machine could simulate. And then with a tap on my shoulder our free fall was over.

As Mario yanked the cord on our parachute, we shot straight up into the air with a powerful force. Then suddenly everything was completely silent. We sat still in the air and it was the most peaceful feeling that I had ever felt in my life. For that brief period of time everything was right with the world. We were surrounded by nothing but beautiful blue sky. The wind that had been pounding us for a couple of minutes became completely silent. I wanted to bottle up that feeling of complete peacefulness and cherish it forever. It was at that time that I understood and envied the wonderful life that a bird must live. You are above everything. No one can harm you, no one can touch you. You are the king.

Mario interrupted the silence and I came back to earth.

"So what did you think?" he asked.

"That was the greatest feeling of my life."

We glided through the sky and practiced our stops and turns. Mario labeled me as an excellent student and then decided that he wanted to speed up our descent. We began turning to the right, dropping quickly turn after turn after turn. I really enjoyed the free fall, but I didn't really like spinning around and around.

"Mario, I don't feel so good" I said.

"What is the matter, are you feeling dizzy?"

Little did I know that one of Mario's greatest thrills in life is trying to get first time jumpers to puke on the way down. As much as I loved the free fall, I hated this.

"Hey man, can we stop the spinning?" I asked.

"I guess" he replied.

THE ULTIMATE CHALLENGE

He pointed to our target and said that he would line us up for the landing but that I needed to pull down hard on the handles to land us softly. Mario wanted a perfect landing. We quickly approached the target landing sight and I pulled down on the handles to slow us down. I let up and then pulled down again as we softly collided with the ground. Ron Craig was there and he quickly approached me to get my reaction. I said that it was great as quickly as I could while trying to hold in the vomit. Mario unstrapped me and I walked away from the landing area as fast as I could while trying to control the nausea. It passed quickly and I was safely on the ground. As my nausea disappeared the excitement returned as I watched my friends approach.

One by one they landed, each as thrilled as I was. We had just experienced one of the most amazing things that a person could ever try. We easily could have sat down and talked about our jumps for the rest of the afternoon but there was no time for that, we were losing. Our RV was now fixed and waiting for us. Eric, Drew and Jason took off their jump suits as quickly as they could and we sprinted to our vehicle. We were getting close to Stone Mountain Georgia and we knew that we were about an hour behind the rednecks, so the pressure was mounting. Our directions were written out for us. We were to cross the bridge over into Memphis, then drive down to Mud Island where we would board a boat and float down the Mississippi River to Vicksburg Mississippi.

Chapter 28

The drive was not a long one, less than ten miles. I had driven the route many times while traveling from Texas to my hometown in Tennessee. It always lifted my spirits to see Memphis and this time was no different. I always loved leaving Arkansas because there was really nothing to see on the interstate and the ride was horrible with bump after bump. Crossing the bridge into Memphis is a beautiful sight. The Mississippi River is below you and Mud Island is to your left with some of the most beautiful homes that you will ever see. You can also see the Pyramid, a very unique architectural masterpiece and also home to the Memphis Tigers basketball team. To the right is downtown Memphis. The majority of the buildings are older with the most beautiful being the historic Peabody Hotel. When you enter the Peabody, you are taken back in time with a majestic lobby that reminds you of the 1920's.

Thankfully for us, the traffic was light as we entered Mud Island and we enjoyed the largest crowd since the beginning of the race. About three thousand people had gathered to cheer us on as we parked the RV about fifty yards from the river where our boat was waiting. As we exited the vehicle, the crowd noise was deafening. Our blood was already racing through our veins from skydiving but the applause was taking us to a new level of adrenaline. We jumped out and jogged along a trail of people as cameras flashed and security guards held the crowd in place. The crowd formed a trail on both sides to clear a path. We were almost to the boat when I recognized a familiar face.

Traci Brooks was there, cheering us on. I had known Traci for most of my life and she was one of Susan's best friends. Traci was a beautiful blond that was very easy to pick out of a crowd. She had not aged a day since I saw her over eight years before. She wore a tight red skirt that highlighted her shapely curves. She was the all American girl. She was the Valedictorian of our senior class in high school. Now she was the chief resident of a children's hospital in Memphis. She had brains, beauty and a wonderful personality to go with it. I decided that a few seconds wouldn't kill us so I ran over to greet her.

We hugged and exchanged greetings and then I slowly leaned over and whispered in her ear "How far ahead are they?"

"About forty five minutes" she answered. "Good luck."

I was still holding her in my arms when I gave her a peck on the cheek and she gave me another tight hug. She gave the best hugs and this one was a little too good. I could feel her body rubbing against mine and the sweet smell of her perfume. I had not been close to a woman in two weeks which seemed like two years. Her hug did something to me that I could not stop. It was so embarrassing when I began feeling movement in certain areas below the belt and I think that Traci could feel it too. I was in a horrible predicament because I was wearing a Reebok jogging suit with boxer briefs so in a matter of seconds, things were popping out that shouldn't have been.

Luckily, I had a very thin workout jacket on so I took it off and tied it around my waist. I saw Traci glance down at my midsection and she started laughing a little.

"See you later" I said and sprinted as quickly as I could to the boat. I was hoping that the movement of my body would shield my embarrassment until I got things under control. I jumped onto the boat, which Drew had already started and quickly took a seat while simultaneously folding my legs in an awkward position. I was breathing hard from the fast sprint and the awful predicament

THE ULTIMATE CHALLENGE

that I had put myself into. I tried my best to play it off by waving to the crowd, hoping that nothing was discovered. My eyes spotted Traci who was waving to the boat, so hopefully she wasn't too offended and would just keep my problem between us.

Drew needed my help in getting out of the dock area and I made up an excuse that I couldn't help because my foot was hurting.

"I can't help it, I need everyone's help so stand up and tell me how much room that I have on your side."

I stood and used one of my arms to shield my embarrassment.

"You are fine over here" I said.

Drew glanced at me as I answered and my secret was no secret any longer. "Man, you must really like the Mississippi River" he said while laughing.

I did not answer him but instead gave him a look that could kill.

Jason heard his comment and also looked at me to see what the joke was about. Jason's eyes opened wide as he too laughed and said "I know that you are happy to see me, but come on, get control of yourself."

I turned a dark shade of red and luckily for me Eric was trying to study a map and paid no attention to us. I hoped that the cameras hadn't picked anything up. There was nothing that I could do, it was just human nature. I surely didn't mean for it to happen.

I had to change the subject in my mind to resolve the problem so that it would go away and then the jokes from my friends would stop also. It was a gorgeous spring day in Memphis and we were only forty minutes behind in the race, so it was time to focus on The Ultimate Challenge.

The Mississippi River is huge! It is hard to appreciate its size unless you are actually on the river. Millions of gallons of fresh brown water are flowing southward heading swiftly towards the Gulf of Mexico. The river current increased the speed of our boat. It made you wonder where in the world did all of this water originate? We felt trapped at Alcatraz, but floating down the Mississippi felt like the definition of freedom. The air flowed through my hair as the sun beat down on my back. We were running at full throttle and breathing down Team Nikes backs. The only problem was that we knew that our boat did not go any faster than theirs, so this was yet another challenge where we were depending more upon a machine than our own strength.

Drew had the most experience on our team of driving a boat so the rest of us kicked back to enjoy the ride. Jason, Eric and I sat in the front, watching our boat cut straight through the flowing water.

"What are we going to do if we don't win this thing?" Jason asked.

"Don't talk like that!" Eric sharply replied. "We are going to win."

"I am not giving up. I'm just asking."

"I really haven't thought about it much" I answered. "I guess we will do the talk show circuit regardless of if we win or lose. And some companies may want us to promote their products."

"That won't last forever" Jason replied. "If we lose, we get nothing."

"Well I would just go back to coaching" Eric answered.

"I need a change anyway" I said. "I want to lead people. My company doesn't listen to anything that I have to say. They could have cared less about my ideas. If we lose, I will just ride out my fifteen minutes of fame and then find a new career."

THE ULTIMATE CHALLENGE

"From the way that you looked when you got on the boat, you could probably work for Viagra" Jason snidely remarked.

Eric looked confused but laughed anyway so I decided to get him. He was such an easy target. "What are you laughing at? If you keep crying every time Little House on the Prairie comes on, you could work for clear eyes."

Jason added "He is small enough that he could probably get a deal working for Pampers!"

That did not amuse our little friend so he went to help Drew navigate the boat. Jason and I quickly joined our teammates as Memphis disappeared behind us. We made our way down the winding river as an Ultimate Challenge boat filled with river experts followed closely behind. They didn't give us advice or navigational tips, but were with us in case of an emergency.

We quickly learned that this part of the trip was not as easy as one might think. We had to zig and zag our way past large barges. The river was huge but so were the vessels that we were passing. Drew was doing a good job behind the wheel but his stress level was high. One wrong move could cost us the race or even worse, our lives. We offered him assistance but couldn't provide any so we decided to leave him alone and return to the front of the boat.

Eric was both a history and geography teacher so he provided us with some background on the river that we were traveling down. "This river is really pretty fascinating" he started.

"Where does all of the water come from?" I asked.

"There are actually twelve different rivers that feed it. There are also a lot of lakes and marshes along the river. There are a bunch of natural levies that have formed from sediment and floods that have occurred."

"That is a good thing, right?" Jason asked.

"Well, it is good and bad. The problem is that sediment has also formed on the bottom of the river so all of this farmland can flood really easily like it did about eight years ago. The seafood industry is also concerned because the marshes are slowly disappearing."

"Why" I asked.

"There are a lot of opinions, but it is a combination of dams, man-made chemicals, pollution and new waterways that oil companies have built. But it is the history of the river that really fascinates me."

Eric was in his element. He loved to teach and we had never seen this side of him. I was amazed at the wealth of information that he was delivering in his South Georgia accent. He was so into his history lesson that he was standing on the front of the boat and pointing as he talked. Jason and I were attentive students, amazed by the professional manner that he was delivering his message. He wasn't just a jock, he really cared about his profession.

"I bet you guys didn't know this" he continued, "but we acquired the Mississippi River in the Louisiana Purchase. It was a major means of travel for Native Americans and the French. Then it was a major means for imports and exports for the United States in the 1800's. Then in the Civil War, the North used the Mississippi River as a major invasion route. Some of the biggest battles of the war were fought on the shores of this river. After the war, railroads started becoming the main means of transportation. But still today, all of these barges that we see are carrying petroleum, chemicals, sand and gravel."

"Well, I must say that I am impressed" Jason said.

"Yeah, this river has a lot of history" Eric answered.

THE ULTIMATE CHALLENGE

"No, we are impressed with you" I replied. "We thought that all you really cared about was coaching."

"That just goes to show you not to assume" Eric proudly answered.

It was starting to get dark and the boat of experts behind us found a place for us to dock for the night. We stopped near Greenville Mississippi. We were halfway to Vicksburg and with the rednecks less than an hour in front of us, we knew that they were still somewhere on the river. Stopping where we did definitely had its advantages. The river experts called for a taxi and within an hour after docking, we were enjoying a steak dinner and rooms at a Hampton Inn. After engulfing my well done New York Strip, we made it back to the room around nine. We were all tired but not ready to sleep so we congregated in Drew's room to shoot the bull for a while.

Chapter 29

"Drew, you should have heard Eric today. He gave me the best history lesson that I have ever gotten" Jason said.

"It is kind of neat to see how we have evolved" Eric replied.

"Yeah, just think about it. If you would have asked anybody that knew us in college what our future would be, the answer would have been depressing" Drew commented.

"We did just enough to get by" I said. "We sewed our wild oats and then sowed them again. We were young, we were stupid but then we were done. I meet people today that are older than I am that still have a need to be wild and crazy. I am through with it."

"Have you ever sat back and thought about how much time that we wasted being hung over" Jason said as he pondered his thought.

"But it was a great time in our lives" Eric replied.

"I agree. But think about it Eric?" I said. "You and I used to sit around every week and wonder why we couldn't meet good girls to date us. Now that you look back, the answer was easy. We partied every weekend. We had no ambition and our house smelled like somebody had died in it."

"Maybe" Drew replied. "But I wouldn't trade it for the world."

"Well, I know that you and Jason have both found true love. Because no good woman in her right mind would have stayed with you through college if it wasn't meant to be" I said.

"You are right about that" Jason said. "Those poor girls went through a lot. We had a mushroom growing in the shower, nobody closed the door when they peed and we had to throw our dishes away twice because they had maggots on them. How sick is that?"

"Oh my God. I forgot about that" Eric answered as he shook his head. "How in the world did we live like that? Do you guys remember that refrigerator from hell?"

"Oh yeah! I remember it" I exclaimed. "One night we were all out at a party down the street and I left early to take a girl back to the house. I really liked her and she was way above my pay grade. It was all set up. We could finally be alone and I could really get to know her better with no interference from anyone. Then I opened the door and the smell knocked me down. I tried to tell her that we needed to leave but she went inside anyway. I don't know what died in that refrigerator but that girl never spoke to me again!"

"Do you guys remember Skamp?" Drew asked as all eyes turned to Eric.

"Don't look at me" Eric demanded.

"That poor dog" Jason said. "He was so scared of Eric that even if he saw you he would pee right where he was.

"Yeah, he peed on the couch, on the chair and anywhere else that he could think of" Drew added.

THE ULTIMATE CHALLENGE

"I lost a girlfriend because of that stupid dog" Eric stated. "She was holding it and all that I did was go up to pet it and it peed all over her. I finally had a good girl that was interested in me and after the dog peed on her it was over."

Everything was good in Team Reebok's camp. We were losing, but we were still together, in it until the end.

"I am just glad that we made it out of college alive" I said.

"You know" Drew said "I am glad that we did all of that partying in college. We got it out of our system. I work with a lot of people that didn't. They go out and get sloshed every weekend, then come back to work on Monday talking about how terrible their lives are."

"Hey, I am with you there" Jason said. "I still drink some but it is nothing like we did back then. I don't see how people do it."

"If you are over thirty and get drunk more than once a week, you are really not happy" Eric said. "There is something missing."

"You know guys, speaking of happy, this whole thing has made me happier than I have been in a long time" Jason said.

"Are you serious?" I asked.

"Yes. I know that some terrible things have happened and we have had some arguments, but I have really enjoyed it."

"Me too" I said. "Family aside, it has been a really long time since I have really wanted something as bad as I want this. Other than my family, I have really been struggling. I haven't really accomplished anything. I am pretty good at my job but it is not what I want to do forever."

"I am the same way. I have been happier in the last two and a half months than I have been in years" Drew said. "But I have a big debt to repay and if we don't win, I don't know what I will do."

"Do I have to tell you guys why we are all happy?" Eric shouted.

"You tell us professor" Jason answered.

"We are happy because we are together again. Our families are great and they make us happy. But really good friends are hard to find. We have this bond and no matter what we do to each other, we are still friends in the end. We would die for each other. We may not see each other for years and still pick up right where we left off. John Simmons realized that, but it was too late for him. That is why he came up with this race."

"You figured that out in Alcatraz didn't you?" Drew asked.

"Yeah and a lot of other stuff that I need to work on."

"You know guys, we are getting down to crunch time" I said. "I can't see this thing lasting much longer."

"I agree. Flying all the way from San Francisco to Memphis made me a little nervous" Drew replied.

"We just have to keep pushing. We need a challenge where we rely on our legs to catch up" Eric stated.

"I think that we are in pretty good shape. They are not that far in front of us" I said while trying to sound enthusiastic.

"Well sitting up all night talking about it isn't going to help us any" Jason said and that was our cue to get some sleep.

THE ULTIMATE CHALLENGE

The king sized bed in my hotel room was a welcomed sight. So was the shower in the bathroom. I took a long hot shower, shaved and was then ready for that comfortable bed. Before getting into the bed, I had to do my hotel bed check ritual. I had to lift the covers and check for bloodstains or pubes before allowing myself to lay on the sheets. I had definitely watched too many special reports on news stations.

I spent my last waking moments thinking of Susan and Thomas. I couldn't wait to see them when the race was finally over. Regardless of the outcome, I would spend the next few weeks with my family to make up for lost time. I had so much to tell Susan. I had experienced a lifetimes worth of adventure in a few short days and she would want to hear every detail.

The next morning began at 5:00 A.M, well before the sun rose. We enjoyed an artery clogging breakfast at Denny's then made our way to the dock to finish our river trip. As we walked to the dock, you couldn't help but notice that the river had a very eerie appearance to it. A light fog hung over the water as the first light of day started to appear. I had always loved traveling by water as a means of transportation. As we traveled down the Mississippi, I was entranced by the flow of the river. I enjoyed staring out over the water, hoping to see something unusual in this huge body of water and the river did not disappoint.

Drew was back at the helm and a little less nervous with the prior day's experience as a notch on his belt. He still said very little so that he could concentrate on his job. Eric had found a small mirror in one of the storage shelves on the boat and he was busy plucking out premature gray hairs out of his head, a task that he would eventually deem hopeless. Jason laid out on a bench near the front of our eighteen foot pontoon boat, trying to continue last night's sleep. I was just enjoying the view with my eyes transfixed on the water.

Chapter 30

I saw it first out of the corner of my eye and knew that it must have been an illusion. A second look with my full focus in that direction proved to me that the impossible was true.

"Shark" I screamed.

Every one of my friends gave me a look that said it was way too early in the morning for such a stupid attempt at a joke.

"Guys, I am not kidding, look!" as I pointed about thirty yards in front of our boat. Everyone looked to appease me but knew that they were falling for a prank. Then to each of their surprise, a fin surfaced out of the water.

"He's right! Look out there!" Eric shouted, as excited as an eight year old seeing Disney World for the first time. Jason was wide awake now and panning his eyes in every direction to spot the shark.

"There it is! I see it!" he proclaimed.

We were heading in the direction where the shark was swimming and as the boat approached, we saw it up close. It was a ten foot long Tiger shark. I had seen a special about them on the Discovery Channel and now remembered that the narrator said that the Tiger shark had actually been spotted several hundred miles upstream in freshwater rivers. I didn't believe him at the time, but there the shark was, right in front of us. The Tiger shark is one of the most aggressive sharks towards people and we were getting to see one up close and personal. We all stared at one of the most feared fish in the sea. Drew was having a fit because he couldn't get a closer look.

"Let's mess with it" Eric shouted as the testosterone level in his body rose to its maximum.

"What do we do?" Jason asked.

Eric needed bloody fresh fish but none was available so he did the only other thing that he could think of. He grabbed an eight foot long metal pole, leaned over the side of the boat and started pounding the water with the pole. The shark that had been circling our boat disappeared and we were sure that Eric had scared it away. Jason, Eric and I all stood on the side of the boat, hoping that the shark would reappear. To our disappointment, we stood in silence and saw nothing. Our boat continued moving forward and the river showed us nothing and our adventure appeared to end without a climax. Eric wasn't giving up so he continued the process of pounding the water with his pole. Jason and I lost hope and interest so we turned around to take a seat. Eric finally gave up also and stopped his pounding because his energy was zapped. "That was probably a stupid idea anyway" Jason said. I nodded in agreement.

The shark struck out of nowhere. In an awesome display of power, quickness and deception, the beast sprung out of the water to each of our surprise and horror. The sharks head was bigger than a recliner with several rows of menacing sharp knives for teeth. It attacked the pole that Eric was still holding. The pole had been dangling in the water on the side of the boat. The jolt of the pole caused by the sudden attack caused Eric to lose his balance. His gut reaction was to grip the pole for leverage which actually was the worst possible thing that he could do. The shark's mighty jaws surrounded the two inch metal pole and then the beast shot down into the water. The end of the pole that Eric was holding

THE ULTIMATE CHALLENGE

lifted him up into the air. Eric's legs kicked wildly, trying to stay on the ground as his pole was beginning to disappear into the water. Jason and I were no help as we were paralyzed in fear and disbelief. We were watching the events unfold in slow motion as Eric was struggling to stay in the boat. It was evident that the pole was going into the river, the only question was if Eric was going with it.

Jason and I finally reacted as Eric regained his senses and let go of the pole. He grabbed the side of the boat as he landed but his legs landed in the river. Jason and I quickly each gave him a hand and pulled him swiftly back into the boat. He then crawled to the middle of the pontoon where he tried to catch his breath.

"Tell me that didn't just happen" he said between gasps of air.

Jason and I ignored our friend in his time of need. We stared out at the river, each a few feet away from the side of the boat, trying to hopefully not see another glimpse of the shark. It was nowhere to be found. The eminent danger was over and Drew laughed as he commanded our tiny ship.

"Sharks don't live in the river" Eric said, trying to make some kind of sense of his near death experience. "Sharks are salt water fish. How did that happen?"

I could have told him about the television show that I had seen but I knew that it would do him no good for now. He didn't need to know that it was probably a Tiger shark that was more aggressive than any other. "That is just crazy" I said.

From that point forward, we looked at the river differently. Things have changed over time on land so that people can live safely, but life in the water has never changed. It was dangerous and mysterious. No member of Team Reebok would ever step foot in an ocean or river again.

We continued our trip with hopes of reaching Vicksburg with every turn. Unlike the interstate, there were no mileage markers to show us our progress.

Navigational maps were a foreign language to us so we stayed as close to the center of our massive liquid interstate as possible, only veering to the side for the gigantic barges that we encountered. There were hundreds of forks in the river but the guessing was easy, as our road was the biggest. Eric recovered from the scare with a newfound respect for all things swimming. I had been on the river long enough. My patience was wearing thin. The end was coming, I could feel it. I wanted for us to decide the outcome, not a car or a boat. We needed that chance, a chance to stare our enemies in the face and promise them that they would lose. It would be easy to say what if this didn't happen, or what if that didn't happen, but it did us no good now. We were clearly in better physical shape than the other team but they still enjoyed a comfortable lead. We had to make our move soon to have any chance at winning.

After four more hours on the river, we finally reached our destination. The city of Vicksburg finally showed itself to us. The casinos along the water's edge were such a welcomed site for us because we knew that we would be parting ways with the water. As we pulled up to the dock, Eric was the first one out of the boat. He offered us no assistance in securing the vessel, but instead he hugged the ground as if it was his best friend.

We ran to the RV allowing only a polite smile to the small crowd that had gathered. There was no time for pleasantries now, we were all business. Eric beat us to our vehicle and had his finger on the play button so as not to waste a single precious second. John Simmons appeared on the screen once more. He had a sparkle in his eye and a grin on his face. He looked healthy and happy. He didn't look like a man on his death bed. He had given us the chance to live the adventure of our dreams. He had also given millions of people watching a chance to live a fantasy through us. We listened attentively as he spoke.

Chapter 31

"Well guys, this is the last time that you will see me. I hope that The Ultimate Challenge has been as exciting for you to play as it was for me to dream up. You have one last challenge for all of the marbles. You are to drive to Atlanta, Georgia, the steps of the capitol building to be exact. From there, I have a route for you that will take you 26.2 miles to the top of Stone Mountain where the winner of The Ultimate Challenge will be crowned. That's right boys, you are all running a marathon. It is not going to be easy, but after all, it is one hundred million dollars that you are running for. Put on a good show and good luck!"

Eric raced to the driver's seat and we peeled out of the parking lot with the great state of Georgia on our minds.

"I knew that it was going to be hard, but a marathon?" Jason asked in disbelief.

"This is the greatest thing that could happen to us" I said. "We have a lot of ground to make up, so the longer the race, the better our chances are."

"You are right Mark. The biggest advantage that we have on those guys is our legs" Drew replied.

"But it is a marathon" Jason reiterated.

"Calm down. We will pace ourselves and do the best that we can. If we need to walk, we will walk" Drew explained to calm Jason's nerves.

I took a seat in the captain's chair behind Eric, opened a bottle of water and did some quick math in my head. Let's see here, they are forty five minutes ahead of us, give or take a few. The race is 26.2 miles long. If you break that down, then we need to run about two minutes faster per mile than the rednecks. The truth is that we are not that much faster than them, not two minutes per mile for 26.2 miles.

I began to panic on the inside, thinking that Team Nike's lead was insurmountable. Then my calm side took control. I had to think about it. Nothing had gone as planned for the entire race. The team that wins is the team that does not run out of gas. The most important thing for us was to not panic. The marathon had taken us by surprise. Our longest run during training was only half of that distance. It takes years for some people to train for a marathon. It had been almost a week since we had hiked the Appalachian Trail. The most physical thing that we had done since then was sprint fifty yards to our vehicle. This was going to be very difficult.

Our drive would take us through Meridian Mississippi, Birmingham Alabama and then onto Atlanta and it would be pretty hard to get lost because interstate 20 took us right where we needed to go. The drive would take about six and a half hours and with one quick stop for gas, we were hoping to be running by 5:30 eastern time. Because of Drew's heroics in driving the boat, we decided that he could rest all of the way to Atlanta.

Drew took a seat beside me as Jason kept Eric entertained up front.

"What do you think our chances are?" Drew asked.

"I think that we have a decent chance" I replied.

"You know that I am dead if we lose, right."

THE ULTIMATE CHALLENGE

"If we lose, which we won't, we will find the money for you to pay your debts" I assured him.

"That is nice of you to say, but the deadline for me to pay is the end of the race!"

"Drew, hopefully those guys aren't stupid. They know that you will get endorsement deals after the race, no matter who wins. They need for you to be healthy in order to get their money."

"I hope you are right" he nervously answered. "I know one thing. I am finished with gambling. That's it. I have had enough!"

"I am glad to hear you say that. When we win, the money that you owe will be a drop in the bucket."

"I have no idea how I let it get that high. I just got so caught up in it and thought that my luck had to turn at some point."

"That is something that you have got to learn how to control. Especially if we win, because people will be coming at us from every direction with investment ideas and who knows what else" I said.

"And my answer is no!" Drew emphatically stated. "How are we going to approach this marathon?" Drew asked.

"The key is our mental strength. We need to know our limits and stay within them. We just have to believe that in the end, we are the stronger team. We have to stay together and watch each other."

"We have to make sure to leave our egos behind" Drew added. "If someone is getting weak, we will walk for a while. That is so much better than one of us collapsing."

I agreed "We have to keep our minds focused on the goal. We need to remember the dreams that we have and our families waiting for us at the end. That will get us through the tough times."

"What if we have to pee or even worse, take a dump? Drew asked.

"I have no idea. I guess you just do it on the side of the road and go on" I answered. "We have to stay hydrated, that much I do know.

The drive that we were making was very familiar to me because we had driven the same route to attend John Simmons funeral. What an irony it was for me. The first time that I traveled on I-20, I was attending his funeral. Now, I was trying to win his fortune. I stared out of the window as we crossed the state line into Alabama. I was tired, we all were, but those thoughts were the farthest thing from our minds. Within a matter of hours, our lives were going to change forever. We were either going to be living a life of luxury or wondering where next month's rent was coming from. Every person reaches turning points in their life but very rarely does someone see such a dramatic contrast staring them in the face. Our big moment was just around the corner. Our destiny was in our hands.

My destiny depended not only upon myself but also on my friends. Our mutual effort would determine our fate. We had been through a lot in The Ultimate Challenge. We had supported each other when we had to and fought at times when we didn't need to. But when the time came, I always knew that we would come together to reach our goal. If we won or lost, our friendship would always remain the same.

To my bewilderment, I dozed off and missed the entire state of Alabama and part of our drive through Georgia.

"Mark, wake up, we have got a race to win" Drew said.

"What? Where are we?" I asked in an alarmed and confused voice.

THE ULTIMATE CHALLENGE

"We are going to be there in an hour" Jason said from behind the wheel.

"You slept for three hours" Eric said.

"I'm sorry guys"

"It's all right. We thought that you might want to wake up and prepare" Drew answered.

"That is crazy. I never sleep in the car" I said. I was a little alarmed but we still had plenty of time to get ready. Jason continued driving as the rest of us stretched our legs in every way that we knew how. I put on an extra pair of socks to try to prevent blisters from popping up. The time was starting to speed up as we were preparing for something that we had never done.

"What kind of pace do you think that we should set? Eric asked the group.

"Do you think that we could sustain a ten minute mile" I asked.

"That is fine with me" Jason answered without taking his eyes off of the road.

"I don't want to go any slower than that" Drew added.

"Okay. It is set then" Eric said in a voice of finality.

Five minutes later the phone rang and it was Ron Craig. "Mark, how are you guys doing?" he asked.

"We are fine Ron. How far ahead of us are they?"

"Don't you wish that I could tell you?" he cheerfully answered. He continued "A police escort is going to lead you guys into Atlanta so that you won't have any disturbances. Your path is roped off near the capitol and security will be with you at all times. The race will end in darkness but Stone Mountain is lit up like a Christmas tree so don't worry about it. Do you have any questions?"

"None that you can answer" I replied.

"Good. Then I will see you at the top."

"Did he say anything useful?" Jason asked.

"A police escort is going to be picking us up soon. That is about it. Just stay right behind them" I answered.

Chapter 32

As we inched closer to Atlanta the traffic started getting heavier and so did our burdens. I was nervous, very nervous. The solo in Las Vegas and jumping out of a plane was a walk in the park compared to this. Being nervous was good in a way. I kind of relished the underdog role. I certainly would love to be winning this thing but the thought of the other team looking over their shoulder for us every thirty seconds made my blood start pumping. Because there was going to be a time, I didn't know when, but there would be a time when they looked back and their worst nightmare would be coming true. We would be gaining fast and their legs would weaken. I just felt it in my bones.

I was awake now and my competitive fire was burning. As I peered around the vehicle, the same look was on every face. Winners relish the moment before game time. This was our race to win and no one was going to take it away. We had been through too much not to take home the prize. The nerves in the pit of my stomach transformed into adrenaline. And when the six car brigade of Georgia state troopers surrounded the RV with sirens blowing and lights flashing, the adrenaline turned into energy.

As the skyline of Atlanta appeared before us, we had one last team meeting.

"O.K. guys, we all know what we have to do" I started.

"Our adrenaline is running high, so we have to remember that this is a marathon" Eric added.

"And if someone needs to walk, just say it. Don't try to be a hero unless we are a mile from the finish line" Jason added.

"One last thing guys" Drew said. "Win or lose, this has been one hell of a ride and I will never forget this time we had together."

As we approached the state capitol, the crowd grew thick. People were everywhere waving signs in the air and shouting. Camera crews and photographers were busy trying to find the best possible angle to capture the beginning of the run. It was like a Christmas parade and we were the float with Santa Claus on it. To our delight, Atlanta's finest were out in full force and they easily cleared a path for us. As we exited the RV, the crowd noise rose several decibels, with a lot of cheers and a few boos mixed in. An announcer blared out of the surrounding speakers that Team Reebok had arrived and their final leg of The Ultimate Challenge was underway. I glanced quickly at the shiny dome on the top of the state capital then abandoned all other sightseeing for another day. We waved once to the crowd and were on our way, jogging to meet our destiny. The taped off route was easy to follow as a large crowd of thousands had gathered to witness a piece of the action.

My legs felt strong, like a champion thoroughbred's. Everyone wanted to run faster but Eric insisted on our ten minute mile pace. The evening was pleasant, about sixty five degrees, perfect weather for a twenty six mile run. We stayed in the middle of our six foot wide path to avoid any accidental mishaps. We ran in pairs with Eric and Jason in the lead and Drew and I close behind.

I felt like I was running on air. It was good to be using my legs again. We had trained so hard to prepare for this race, so it was very fitting that it would be decided by our physical strength. I stared straight ahead while we ran, but the tremendous crowd was a wonderful diversion from the feat that we had in front

THE ULTIMATE CHALLENGE

of us. My goal was to distract my mind for as long as possible from the fact that I was running the longest race of my life. I wasn't worried about my legs, I knew that they would carry me for as long as I wanted to go. If I had a problem, it would be my lungs. Two months of intense training had whipped my lungs into shape, but I wasn't sure how they would react to a marathon.

Many spectators had been waiting for hours to see The Ultimate Challenge. The day had turned into a huge party for most. The Atlanta police were doing a fine job of controlling the crowd but several groups had been drinking all day. We had our share of fans, but so did Team Nike. We passed several people with banners, some encouraging and others that were not appropriate for a child to see.

About three miles into the race, we were beginning to work up a sweat and reach a comfort level in the group with everyone in sync in our strides. We then noticed a huge banner that was draped across an overpass. As we approached it, our comfort level disappeared.

The banner said "If you want to live, you will lose the race."

The security force around us noticed the banner just after I did and they scattered about on full alert. Six motorcycle cops surrounded our group with their eyes peeled on the spectators. My initial reaction was one of disgust. It was just some psycho trying to cash in on a few seconds of fame. Then my thoughts turned to fear. What if the rednecks have people working for them? People that they pay to deter us. We were treading on dangerous ground. People have been murdered for a lot less money than we were racing for.

I didn't speak to my teammates, as we all were much more concerned with saving our precious breath than wasting it on talking. This was just one more obstacle that we would have to overcome. Every innocent fan now could be a threat to us. The noise of the crowd was now making me a little nervous as the threat on our lives had put them in control of the race. Someone could have a gun and never be seen. We were passing thousands of people and I was sure that at least one of them would do whatever it took to make sure that we lose the race.

My thoughts were no longer focused on winning, now I was hoping just to survive. As we passed the four mile mark, my mind was racing. I was feeling the warning signs of a panic attack. My legs were weakened and felt like spaghetti. I wasn't sure if they could hold my weight and I felt like I could pass out at any moment. It was a feeling that I had experienced before, usually while walking in shopping malls. It was a feeling that at any moment my legs would collapse. I started getting tunnel vision, the crowd blurred and I wasn't able to focus on anything.

"Mark, are you O.K." Drew asked. "Mark!" he shouted.

"Yeah, I am all right." I answered without a glance at Drew.

Jason and Eric looked back at me with concern written on their faces. I nodded at them and they took it as a sign that I was fine. I knew that I was in trouble and my mind was the only thing that could save me.

"Get it together Mark" I said to myself. I began thinking of things that made me happy. I knew that I was near my wife and son. I started to picture their faces and what they were doing as they waited for the race to end. I knew that I would see them soon. Then I started to think about our journey and all that we had been through to get here.

The cell phone ring woke me up from my daydreaming and once again I heard the noise of the crowd. I answered it in mid-stride.

"Hello."

THE ULTIMATE CHALLENGE

"Mark, it is Ron Craig. We found the guys that hung the banner. It was just a couple of stupid kids, so there are no worries."

"Thanks" I replied and relayed the message to my much relieved team. With the magic of a cell phone, my legs were back under me and Team Reebok could once again focus on the race. The crowd became my friends again and all was right with the world. We were five miles into the marathon and I felt like I could run forever. The panic attack was behind me and nothing could stop us now.

I was no running expert, but I did know a little bit about my own mind. I always ran my best when my mind was a million miles away. If we won the race, I was going to be a very wealthy man. Twenty five million dollars after taxes was unfathomable. My mom and dad could retire. I could travel around the country and see my favorite sports teams play with great seats. I could start a charity that contributed to the American Cancer Society in honor of my fallen comrade. I could drill wells in the Sahara desert for the poor people that have to walk two days to get drinking water. I could help feed the hungry in my hometown. But the greatest feeling of all would be not having to worry about money. It would be fantastic not to have to carefully watch the checkbook every month. I would love to not have to tell Susan that we really needed to watch our spending. It would be great not to have to worry about sales numbers every single month and always fear the loss of my job. I would never lose sleep at night over financial worries. My parents and siblings wouldn't have to live from one month to the next. I was running for all of those reasons.

At the eight mile mark I was working up a really good sweat. The cool Georgia air was allowing oxygen to flow easily through my nose and mouth and into my lungs. I had absolutely no signs of fatigue and my friends looked as strong as I did. There was no sign of Team Nike but it was still early. We were the hunters and they were the hunted. They were out of site but we were hunting them. In the end, the escaped prisoner always gets caught.

Chapter 33

I did not dare speak to my teammates because I had no idea about how much energy it might zap. So it was back to daydreaming. My mind turned to my childhood and my greatest running experience as a young teenager. I was in the eighth grade and decided to run track to stay in shape for basketball. The track coach was also the basketball coach and he was the toughest coach that you will ever meet. Coach Taylor was his name and it didn't take a genius to figure out that his background was in the military. His philosophy was simple. The team that was in the best shape would win. Our track practice was also very simple. He would load the team up in a big yellow bus and drive us out into the country. He would order us to get out of the bus and we would run behind it for miles and miles. And back then, for some reason, I loved it. Maybe it was because we were outside which was much more fun than running laps in a gym. Coach Taylor was famous for making us run laps during basketball season. If you did something wrong, then you run one hundred laps. If you did something else wrong, you do one hundred push-ups. He made us wear embarrassing toboggans on our heads whenever we were outside during basketball season. He didn't allow us to drink soft drinks during basketball season. If you got caught drinking a soft drink or not wearing your toboggan, you guessed it, you ran one hundred laps around the gym. I despised Coach Taylor at the time but I was in the best shape of my life. He was teaching us something that I didn't appreciate until much later in life. He was instilling discipline in his players. Discipline that would help us graduate from college and succeed in our careers. I owe a lot to that man. He taught me more than any book ever did. I was running the next mile for Coach Taylor.

The ten mile mark came and went without me even noticing. We were out of the city and the crowd was thinning out. It was us, the camera truck leading our way and the motorcycle cops draped to our side. Jason was directly in front of me and his shirt was soaked with sweat. I had another sixteen miles of staring at his greasy butt. I focused my attention on the cameras in the truck and began to realize how many people were actually watching our every move. Watching four guys jog for twenty six miles could not be very exciting. But if everything that we heard was correct, millions of people were watching us run. They had followed us daily from beginning to end. They had witnessed our ups and downs, the frustrations and elation that we had experienced. The fans knew us now. They knew our personalities and character. The viewers had decided on their favorites and long before today they had picked a team to cheer for.

The cameras had become a normal part of our surroundings since The Ultimate Challenge began. I never really thought about how I looked or what I said. To do so would have been exhausting. Someday, I would enjoy watching our adventure from a viewer's perspective, but no time soon. Being in front of a camera was much different than I had imagined. I don't know what I expected, but life goes on as normal. You just know that other people are watching what you are doing. There was never a great feeling inside of me that things on television are larger than life. Nothing changed.

My only other brush with television had come when I was a senior in high school. A friend of mine talked me into taking a trip to Nashville to be an audience extra for a Joan Jett rock video. We showed up at the Opryland amusement park that morning along with about two hundred other people. We figured that we would hear her sing the song a few times and if we were lucky, we would be in the video. All of the other fans were dressed in black leather outfits. Me, I wore my Georgia Bulldogs sweatshirt.

THE ULTIMATE CHALLENGE

We waited for two hours for Joan Jett to make her first appearance. The song was called "Little Liar" and I will die a happy man if I never hear it again. We had to stand up and sway our hands each time that she played the song. By the end of a twelve hour day, I was exhausted and wished that I had not gone.

About two months later, I started receiving call after call at my parent's home. My goofy face was actually on the video. There was a solo shot of me for about two seconds. Everyone said that I looked drunk but the reality was that I only appeared that way from hearing that dreadful song for twelve straight hours. "Little Liar" was the most popular video on MTV for about a month and I was the big man on campus at my high school. Then, just like Joan Jett, my video disappeared forever. I guess no big Hollywood producers wanted me because the phone calls stopped very suddenly. Courtney Cox got her big break in a Bruce Springsteen video. But hey, I'll admit it, I am no Courtney Cox.

We were twelve miles into the race and I was starting to feel the burn in my legs. We passed a group of five drag queens with Team Reebok posters, which was a great bit of comic relief for me.

"Eric, there is your fan club" I said.

He only responded with a shut your mouth face. My legs were holding up despite the burn but my shoulder was aching. I had surgery on the shoulder seven years prior because I had dislocated it twice. Now it was hurting. I felt a dull painful ache. I massaged the shoulder with my left hand as we ran, then decided to give up and just deal with the pain. I limited the movement of my arms and tried to lower my shoulder a bit to ease the tension on it. I could deal with it.

Chapter 34

I tried once again to take my mind away from the race and I saw a cute little four year old girl who was waving to us as we passed. She reminded me of a precious child that I met as a teenager. One summer I went on a mission trip to an impoverished area in Michigan. The men on the mission would be constructing a new church for the area residents. My group would be holding a bible school to teach the young children of the area about God. On the first day, I met a little girl named Sarah that would change my life forever. Sarah had sandy blond hair and dark skin. Her clothes were old and worn but she didn't know it. Her shoes had holes in them but she was the most beautiful child that I had ever seen. Sarah was shy but her smile lit up a room. By the second day, she sat in my lap whenever she could. She was only comfortable sitting in my lap and she devoured the attention that I was giving her. I learned that Sarah's dad had left the family when she was a baby. Her mom did the best that she could but she could barely make ends meet. It broke my heart to see this precious child so starved of love. I promised myself that day that if I was ever lucky enough to find a wife, I would be with her forever.

We had completed fifteen miles of our twenty six mile race so we had eleven to go. I decided that I was going to run the next mile for Sarah. If we were lucky enough to win the race, I made a commitment to myself that I would help single moms and impoverished children so beautiful kids like Sarah could have a better childhood.

At the seventeen mile mark, we still saw no sign of Team Nike. The anxiety began to creep into my mind, what if we never catch them? There was no way that we could run any faster. It was remarkable that we had maintained the pace that we had. My legs were starting to send me signals that they were getting tired. They were beginning to feel heavier as the road was starting to take its toll. My breathing was labored as I was having to work to bring enough oxygen into my body to satisfy my weary lungs. My body was begging for a rest but I was unable to meet the request. I was either going to finish this race or die trying.

After eighteen miles, we still hadn't seen the rednecks and I was in pain. It was very difficult but I managed to take my mind away again. I thought of my lovely wife. I vividly remember the very first day that I saw Susan. We were in the eighth grade and I was walking outside of the gym. As I walked past the gym, I peeked into the open door to catch a glimpse of the pretty girls that were inside. I glanced inside as I passed then stopped in my tracks, stepped back and did a double take of a beautiful girl that I had never seen before. It was Susan's first day at our school and I was immediately interested in her. Through a series of notes that I left in her locker, I became her boyfriend for two months which is a lifetime for an eighth grader. Her beautiful tanned skin and beautiful big blue eyes stole my heart and she became the first big crush of my life.

We remained friends in high school but my feelings remained the same. She blossomed into a gorgeous young woman but I had her on my unattainable list. She dated a series of losers as many young girls do and we lost touch until our five year high school reunion. She was one of the first people to greet me at the door and my attraction to her returned immediately. My confidence level had risen during our five years apart and I wasn't going to let her get away again. We began dating after the reunion and fell madly in love soon after. She is even more beautiful now than the first day that I saw her and she is waiting for me at the end of this race. I am going to run the next mile for Susan.

THE ULTIMATE CHALLENGE

By the time that we hit the twenty mile mark, our pace was beginning to slow down. Every member of Team Reebok was drained and our legs were weakening. Our strides were not as smooth and we were struggling to catch our breath. I was no longer gliding gracefully, but instead my feet were pounding the ground with every step. The hard pavement was jarring my knees and testing my endurance. The end was near but we were too weary to be motivated by the finish line. We had endured twenty miles without an injury, at least until then.

I noticed Drew's limp out of the corner of my eye and before I could speak he had completely stopped and fell to the ground, writhing in pain. I stopped immediately and almost fell down myself from dizziness. After balancing myself, I sat down next to Drew. A medic jumped out of the camera truck to tend to our teammate.

"What is wrong?" we asked as Drew clutched his left foot.

"I stepped on a nail and it is stuck in my foot" he answered as he rocked back and forth in pain. The medic heard his response and immediately removed his shoe.

"He has got a stone bruise" the medic informed us.

"What does that mean?" Drew asked.

"It means that you can continue but it is going to be very painful" the medic answered.

"Let's go" Drew ordered. "If it is not a nail, I will fight through the pain."

We helped him up and began jogging again. The worst thing that we could have done was stop because our bodies wanted to shut down. My breathing was better but my legs felt like they were made of rubber. Our pace was slow but at least we were moving forward. I felt like a ninety year old man with arthritis as every joint in my body was telling me no.

Drew was jogging with a noticeable limp. A stone bruise is a terribly painful injury to walk on, much less run. It is like walking with a tack stuck in your foot so it was easy to see why Drew thought that he had stepped on a nail. Now he had to endure it for six more miles. And he had to do it while we were trying to catch an opponent that we could not even see yet. The mountain that we were trying to climb just became steeper. Drew didn't complain and we were running at a pretty decent pace but his face told the story. All of a sudden my aches and pains were not so bad any more. I wanted to help him but there was nothing that I could do. So we continued on more slowly now, with our dream starting to fade away.

At the twenty-two mile mark, darkness was beginning to take over. Our light was fading fast as evening gave way to night. We were near the finish but still thousands of paces away. We could see Stone Mountain which was both good and bad. Our families were near but there was still no sign of Team Nike. Our path was well lit and the crowd was growing bigger. Every spectator that we passed was urging us on. Drew was dealing better with his stone bruise and with four miles to go, we were back to a brisk run.

My legs were gone, the only thing that kept me going was adrenaline and desire. The crowd grew larger with every step that we took and the cheering fans were the medicine that we needed. When we were almost at the point of collapse, our bodies amazed us. It was time to reach down, deep into your soul, and pull something out of it to keep you going. This was gut check time. A time when ordinary people quit and go home, but we weren't ordinary people and The Ultimate Challenge was no ordinary race.

Chapter 35

"Look!" Eric screamed with all of the energy that his exhausted body could muster. His right index finger pointed weakly in front of us.

About half a mile ahead of us we could barely make out the lights of another camera truck. It was stopped! The truck was not moving and a large crowd had gathered around it. Without a word exchanged between the four of us, our pace immediately quickened. We had a bounce in our step that had been missing for miles. This was our big chance. This was the only chance that we had left. It was hard not to sprint into the lead but we knew that doing so could cost us the race. We ran ahead, praying with each step that the truck would not move.

Thoughts of winning the race were once again alive. If we could just get the lead. If we got the lead there was no way that we would relinquish it. There were only three miles to go in the race and we had a chance to take the lead that we had been chasing for days. A three mile race for one hundred million dollars. I was no longer feeling the exhaustion that had made the past hour the longest of my life. My legs were no longer my focal point, it was the rednecks camera truck.

We were about fifty yards from the truck when it began moving again. The crowd of thousands was sent into a complete frenzy when they saw the event unfolding. We were numb with anticipation and the sweet taste of victory just inches in front of our face. We were running strong and hard. Our feet were pounding the pavement in unison as our confidence level rose with every step. The rednecks camera truck was moving but not as fast as ours.

We were right on their butts when they realized what was happening. With two miles to go in The Ultimate Challenge we pulled even with the other team. We ran to the left of the rednecks and one quick glance told me that they were in trouble. Their faces had an expression of panic written all over them. They sped up, not allowing us to pass them. They were running wildly with their arms flailing about while trying to maintain the lead. We, on the other hand, had a strong confident stride. We had worked all day for this moment and now we were going in for the kill.

Team Nike tried their best to maintain the lead by staying with us for a quarter of a mile. Their legs were weaker than their hearts and with less than two miles to go, we finally regained the lead. We didn't let up after overtaking them. We painfully maintained our pace. The Team Reebok supporters cheered wildly as we passed. The deafening noise of our fans was feeding our battle tested legs. Our lead widened with every stride as the crowd continued to grow. We entered Stone Mountain Park to a sea of cameras. Tons of bulbs were flashing as we passed. It looked like a lightning bug convention.

The end of the race was lifting our spirits but the huge rock that we had to climb was staring us in the face. A marathon is 26.2 miles. We were about to conquer the 26, but the point two was what I was worried about. Team Nike was over one hundred yards behind us with a mile to go but I wasn't sure if we had the strength to make it up the mountain. Just put one foot in front of the next until the race is over. I didn't wave at the fans but they were helping me. Our pace had slowed once again as we approached the base of our climb. I was so tired that my mind was not processing the things that I was trying to think about. Every member of my team was close to collapsing. I tried to think of my family being just minutes away but I had lost my ability to focus.

THE ULTIMATE CHALLENGE

We attacked the base of the mountain as fiercely as we could. Every step upward was difficult. Every step caused a burn in our thighs. It felt like a heating pad had been wrapped around my legs. My feet were pounding and the blisters that had formed were stinging. The skin around my blisters was gone and I was running on raw meat. The trail was not smooth. We had to negotiate the rocks, which upset our balance. People were lined on both sides of the trail with hands in the air and voices screaming. I was in another world, unable to hear anything but the pounding of my heart. The lights that formed the trail to the top were blurs to me as sweat was stinging my eyes. I didn't glance at my teammates, they could fend for themselves. I was leading our way slowly up the mountain. It will be over soon. Just keep on going for a few minutes. Every step was one less that we had to take. That was the only way to look at it. I didn't look back for the other team for fear of falling over.

I climbed up a rock that was about three feet tall. After conquering it, we had thirty yards of smooth uphill sailing with a very gradual slope. I decided to run that thirty yards so that we could get to the top faster. If I only had it to do over again.

Chapter 36

Susan and Thomas were waiting at the top of the mountain with the other wives. They were getting updates every few minutes via an Ultimate Challenge Volunteer. She knew that we had taken the lead but that the race was too close to call. Her nerves were beyond repair as our future was frozen in time. She would either be wealthy or looking for work the next day. It was a horrible contrast and there was nothing that she could do about it. The waiting was the worst part. She could handle the outcome no matter how the race ended, she just didn't know what to prepare for. Thomas was having a great time. He was in amazement while watching all of the people and the lights. He clapped when everyone else did and he remembered something about his mama saying that dada was coming home.

I never even had a chance. The lighting was good, but it would have been impossible to see, even in broad daylight. My face pounded on the rock before I knew that I had fallen. My arms were too weak to brace my fall, so my nose felt the majority of the impact. My right ankle twisted badly and I thought that it might be broken. Blood pulsated from my nose like water from a squirt gun and for a few seconds I watched in shock, unable to help myself. Finally, I removed my sweat soaked shirt and placed it firmly over my nose to control the bleeding. I laid back, staring directly at the starry night.

The crowd acted as a security force as a massive scramble broke out on both sides of the trail. Jason and Drew draped their bodies over me, unsure of how to assist. Eric focused on the crowd and he could tell that something was not as it should be. The Ultimate Challenge security force first surrounded us then sorted out the skirmish in the crowd. The security guys on each side appeared with one prisoner each.

"Hey, those are the same kids that tripped Jason at the beginning of the race!' Eric shouted.

I managed a glance to each side and they were in fact the two young boys that had interfered before. A fifth security guard appeared with a fishing line in his hand. I had been tripped intentionally and the crowd was close to rioting as they figured out what had happened. The security guards had to protect the two boys from the angry mob. Within minutes more security arrived to control the situation. Eric was fuming and I was in agony. My ankle was swelling quickly. Within a minute, it was the size of a grapefruit. Blood had soaked my shirt and was trickling down my bare chest. A medic supplied me with a fresh towel to hold on my nose. I accepted the towel and then motioned for the medic to leave. Eric grabbed one of my arms and Drew took the other. I tried putting weight on the injured ankle and fell again, so I put one arm on Drew and used the other to keep pressure on my bloody nose. We took three awkward steps forward as the fans cheered wildly, trying their best to will us to the top of the mountain.

I noticed the crowd looking behind us and I knew that Team Nike was gaining ground fast.

"Look, Look!" I managed to say through the noise of the crowd.

We were less than one quarter of a mile from the finish line but Team Nike was only fifty yards behind us. At our current pace there was no way to stave them off. I looked at Drew, then Eric, and they both had a look of defeat in their eyes. It was a look of total emptiness. We were so close to the finish line but losing seemed inevitable.

THE ULTIMATE CHALLENGE

I then looked to Jason for a last glance of concession but the glance that he returned was one of insane rage. He walked directly up to me and I had no idea what he was going to do to me. We came face to face with one another but then he lowered his head and grabbed me, lifting me up into the air. My upper torso was draped over his back and he was carrying me on his shoulders.

Jason looked at Drew and Eric with fire in his eyes.

"Let's go" he said and we were off.

Jason wasn't only carrying me, he was leading the way with a pace much faster than we had been going. It was all that Eric and Drew could do to keep up with our hero. The crowd was insane as every single person was now cheering for our team. I was looking directly at the ground and praying while covering my battered nose. I was just along for the ride now. There was nothing that I could do. My nose and ankle were throbbing but they were the least of my worries.

Team Nike was gaining ground as our lead shrunk to thirty yards with the finish line in sight. The mountain levels off at the top and the finish line was sitting at the very middle of the mountain. I could tell when we reached the summit because the ground became smoother.

I looked back at Team Nike and they were in a full sprint with one hundred yards to go.

"Go Jason" I screamed in a voice that was muffled by my broken nasal cavity. "They are right behind us!"

Eric and Drew came up beside us and all three of my teammates shared the weight of my body. It was a sprint to the finish with only a few feet separating the teams. As we approached the finish line, my teammates used every morsel of energy that was left in their bodies. I closed my eyes for the last twenty yards then felt my friends collapse as we crossed the finish line. After a rough landing I opened my eyes to see the final redneck crossing the line.

We had won! We won the race! Susan was the first person to see me as she flung her arms around my bloodied body. I was in shock, total disbelief. Tears were flowing and hugs were exchanged all around the group. Poor Thomas cried when he saw me. The blood was just too much for him to bear. "Da Da?" he questioned as he looked at me in a very confused way. After a minute of me telling him that I was fine, he accepted it.

Ron Craig approached us to offer his congratulations. The crowd was cheering and we all waved to them in thanks. And then, out of nowhere, a ghost appeared. It was John Simmons! He walked over to us and everyone on both teams stopped whatever they were doing and froze.

"You are dead" Eric said in total shock.

"Or so you thought" John answered with the guilty grin that he always had.

Our friend was alive. But nothing made any sense

"Explain yourself please" Jason said as everyone still kept their distance.

"Well boys, about five months ago I created the Expedition Channel. I needed something really good to get things kicked off" he explained.

"So you didn't have brain cancer? I asked.

"Oh yeah. That much is true. I almost died before they even diagnosed brain cancer. Then, the chemo and radiation damn near killed me. When I was going through all of my treatments, I diverted my mind by creating this race. I had to do something because during radiation your face is bolted down on this table and you can't move. So it was a little Bob Marley, James Taylor and the

THE ULTIMATE CHALLENGE

Eagles along with creating this game that got me through it. It was in 2009 and it took years to start feeling half-way normal again. So here we are. And there is another thing that you guys didn't know."

John then waved his hand and out walked Cheryl, John's college sweetheart and she was with two cute little kids.

"When I was in treatment, things were kind of up in the air about whether I would live or die and Cheryl surprised me by coming out to MD Anderson in Houston. We fell in love again, even when I was at my worst. She is a true hero. We got married and have two kids."

"But you gave us all of your money" Drew said.

John had a sly grin on his face. "I gave you some of my money. I am worth a lot more than one hundred million dollars. Plus, I made a lot of it back. You guys paid for a lot of the race yourselves. We had tons of companies lined up to buy advertising."

He looked at each of us. Our team and the other team. "When I was going through cancer treatments and fighting for my life, I realized that my priorities were all wrong. I had made all of this money and lost touch with the people that really cared about me. Cheryl came and it was a God send. But I kept thinking about you guys also. What truly made me happy was the time that I spent with all of you guys. The money was nice, but the bonds that we created were so much more important."

After the initial shock was over, we embraced our friend and his family. We were all still confused, but that was John's way. He had pulled the ultimate gag on all of us and the television audience as well. I was dumbfounded. How did he pull it off? I limped over to the side of the mountain to take a moment for myself. I thought about the past couple of weeks. I thought about Earl the cameraman and John Albert Henley. I thought about the fact that we were now very wealthy. I thought about John still being alive and the fact that what he said about friendship was so true. I thought about Eric realizing how much he loved his wife. Drew started thinking about his spirituality on the trip. Jason learned that he can do anything that he puts his mind to. And me, I won The Ultimate Challenge.

Made in the USA
Lexington, KY
29 May 2019